# AMONG THE MISSING

*K. Wiley Sider*

ISBN: 0692498176
ISBN 13: 9780692498170
Library of Congress Control Number: 2015912031
Devilwood Press, Ellicott City, MD

This book is dedicated to the ghost who lived in my mother's house.

# PROLOGUE

Lucy peered around the corner to see if they were still following her, her heart pounding in her chest, her lungs aching for breath. She scanned the neighborhood of tiny yards with even tinier homes until she spotted them standing in a small group at the end of the street. They looked like they were discussing where she might be and what they would do when they found her. One of them was picking something up from the dirt. Even from a distance, Lucy knew they were rocks, and she knew they were for her.

Things were getting worse again. It had been a long time since Lucy had heard the voices—months, in fact. Nevertheless, Lucy had been hearing them again, like the soft murmur of an audience before a show. If she tried hard enough, she could pick out an individual voice here and there. Sometimes they were talking about her, and that made her feel uncomfortable. She wasn't sure what the voices meant, but she knew from the way the other kids treated her that it wasn't normal. They didn't understand how much harder everything was for her. While they could hear the teacher just fine, Lucy had to strain through all the noise just to understand what was going on. The teasing was harmless during school hours, and for the most part, Lucy was deaf to it. But after school was another story. Most of the kids went home and told their parents about Crazy Lucy; others didn't like how strange she was. It made them afraid, which made them angry. Lucy avoided them the best she could until her aunt came to pick her up from the small bus stop near the school. Usually an adult was nearby, or she could find a place to hide until the kids gave up and went home. But not always. When the voices were especially loud, Lucy didn't always hear them coming until it was too late.

Lucy turned and ran and then felt the sting of the rocks against her bare legs. It wasn't enough to hurt her but more than enough to scare her. She turned to see the small group of kids approaching fast. With fear driving her, Lucy sprinted away from the group, fast enough to avoid the next handful of pebbles they had chucked at her.

As she turned the next corner, she spotted an elderly woman sitting in the shade of an old wooden bus shelter. She'd seen her there before and had said hello on days when someone wasn't trying to beat her up. Lucy hesitated and then walked over when the old woman gave her a kind smile. Inside the shelter, the concrete had a damp smell, despite the heat that baked the pavement beyond the line of shadow. The old woman patted the bench next to her, and Lucy crammed herself into the dark corner, hoping no one would see her.

"You stay here with me, sweetheart," the old woman crooned. She gave Lucy a crinkly smile. "Those kids will just run right by here."

Lucy was doubtful but sat quietly. It was only a moment before she heard the sound of rubber-soled tennis shoes pounding the pavement as her tormentors rounded the corner and charged up the sidewalk behind her. She was invisible behind the worn wood of the shelter. As the sound of footsteps faded away, Lucy let out the breath she'd been holding. Her heart settled as she turned to thank her savior.

"Don't worry about it, dear," the old woman replied. "Just come here and talk to me from time to time. We can wait for our rides together."

Lucy smiled. "I'm supposed to walk home, but my aunt drives right by here after work."

The old woman returned Lucy's smile. "I'm waiting for my daughter. She's late again, as usual."

Lucy sat back and listened as the old woman described a garden she had found, politely murmuring when it seemed appropriate. They didn't notice when a shadow crossed the bright, sunlit pavement just outside the shelter. Both turned to see one of Lucy's tormentors standing there staring at her. Lucy didn't know how long he'd been standing there, but from his expression, she knew it didn't matter. He was staring at her with naked fear, his eyes wide. Lucy opened her mouth to speak, but he turned and ran away.

# ONE

Lucy sat on her back steps and watched as dark clouds rolled over the dry, dusty fields behind her house. Across the bare strip of parched grass that was her own little piece of the world stood a small crabapple tree she had planted the previous fall. Still little more than a twig, it began to whip around in a violent dance with the wind that preceded the much-needed rain. She closed her eyes and raised her face to welcome the cool gust of air. She smiled as the breeze lifted the tendrils that had escaped her ponytail to caress her face. With great effort, she opened her eyes. Lucy checked her watch. Her boyfriend, Jerry, would be over soon, and she needed to get started on dinner. Lucy stood and arched her back, trying to rub the ache out of it. A small seed of resentment crept into her heart as she contemplated the next hour she would have to spend putting something together for Jerry to eat. After eleven months of dating, they had fallen into a pattern that left her coming home from work to make Jerry's dinner, cleaning, and then sleeping... and little else. *I remember when he'd take me out to dinner*, she grumbled as she opened the door and entered the kitchen.

By 10:00 p.m., the storm was blowing hard, and rain was furiously pelting the window over the sink where Lucy stood, drying the last of the dishes. When she was done, she threw down the damp towel in disgust. It was another waste of a dinner, with Jerry quietly finding fault with everything she had prepared. Though he never said anything, the

1

shake of his head or look of distaste on his face was enough to send Lucy back into the kitchen to make him something else. It wasn't until she put the plate of meatloaf on the TV tray in front of him that he smiled and dug in. The three separate dinners for him meant three times the mess for her. It was almost eleven by the time Lucy finished cleaning up and could finally climb the short flight of stairs to her bedroom under the eaves of her small Cape Cod. Jerry had settled in on her couch for some late-night television, so at least she had the bed to herself.

After a brief session in front of the bathroom mirror, Lucy slid under a faded, threadbare quilt she had inherited from her last living relative, an obscure great-aunt remembered only in faded photos of relatives long gone from this world. She closed her eyes and said the same prayer she had been saying her entire life. Never varying, it was simply a prayer of thanks and a hope for forgiveness for the sins of the world. With a humble "Amen," Lucy tucked her hands under her chin and tried to go to sleep, despite the tapping of the rain on the roof above her head.

A short time later, Lucy awoke to a slight headache and a confused babbling of voices. She looked around the small bedroom for the source. Seeing nothing but faded, striped wallpaper and antiquated floral prints in chipped gilt frames, Lucy got up and padded down the stairs to ask Jerry to turn the television down. Lucy poked her head around the corner and was not surprised to see Jerry fast asleep on the couch, his handsome face illuminated by the flickering screen. She was surprised, however, that the sound was already so low that she could barely hear it. Too tired to investigate further, she trudged back upstairs and returned to the warmth under the quilt.

Almost asleep, she heard the voices again, this time louder. Lucy opened her eyes and was startled to see someone sitting next to her on the bed. She sat up with a cry and stared at what looked like a man. Her eyes grew wide, and her heart began to race. She tried to scream, but fear had stolen her voice, so she could only manage a hoarse whisper. Her hands began to shake as she groped the nightstand next to her for something to use as a weapon, her eyes glued to the man in front of her. It took only a moment for her to realize that the man, now standing next to the bed, wasn't entirely whole. In fact, she could clearly see the faint glow of the small nightlight plugged into the wall directly behind him. It was another moment before she realized he was speaking to her.

"I'm terribly sorry to have given you such a fright, but I rather need your help," said the apparition, with the lilt of a British accent. Lucy stared at the man. Despite her shock, she automatically catalogued the details of her intruder. He had a kind, open face (were faces kind?), blue eyes, and short strawberry-blond hair. He was fully dressed in a light denim shirt with a plaid wool car coat, tan pants, and hiking boots. Lucy's reply was unintelligible.

"I perfectly understand your fear," the apparition said. "However, it is entirely unavoidable. You see, you are uniquely qualified to assist me, for, as you can see, I am—well, that is...I am a ghost." The ghost looked at Lucy beseechingly. Then he shrugged and held up his hands, adding, "And you can see me."

With her eyes wide, Lucy slowly shook her head. "I must still be asleep," she murmured to herself. Reaching out, Lucy tentatively placed her hand where the ghost's hand should be. Nothing. She moved to his jacket. Nothing. Placing her hand flat where the ghost's face should be, she wasn't surprised to feel nothing there, either. The ghost peered around her hand and smiled. "See," he said brightly, pointing to his chest, "ghost."

Lucy smiled in return. "Oh yeah," she said, dismissing the specter. "I am definitely dreaming." Then, pulling the quilt up over her shoulder, Lucy rolled over and went back to sleep.

A short time later, Lucy awoke to the slamming of the front door. She thought, *Jerry must be going to his house to sleep.* He was doing that more and more lately. Saddened, Lucy leaned across the bed to turn out the lamp and found herself nose to nose with her ghostly visitor. With another strangled squawk, Lucy sat straight up and stared at the man in front of her.

"Uh, hello, again," he began tentatively. "Please, before you say anything, let me explain." The ghost stood up and began pacing around the small bedroom. "You are not dreaming. As I mentioned before, I am dead, have been for quite some time, thirty years, actually, and, for whatever reason, you are able to see and hear me. Now, I have been looking for someone like you for a long time." Lucy's ghost paused before her. "Before you ask, the answer is yes, there are other people who can see and hear me, but they are few and far between. The last man I found was in India in 1989, and by the time I could find a ghost who spoke Hindi, neither would have anything to do with me." The apparition shook his head. "Perhaps a political issue."

Lucy finally found her voice. "I don't understand. I mean...." Lucy shook her head and then finished softly, her voice shaking. "I don't understand."

Her ghost sighed and sat down next to her. "I don't pretend to, either. All I can tell you is that I am dead, and you are not; when I speak, you can hear me, and that means you may be able to help me."

Lucy rubbed her forehead, where she could feel a headache coming on. Glancing at the small porcelain clock next to the lamp, she was surprised to see it was almost three in the morning. Turning to her persistent guest, Lucy asked, "Do you have a name?"

"Oh yes," the ghost replied quickly. "My apologies. My name is Harry Truman."

"Mr. Truman," Lucy said firmly but politely, "I don't see how I can help you, but I have to get up for work in two hours, and if I don't get at least a little bit of sleep, I'm not going to be able to make it. So if you don't mind, I'd like this dream to be over so I can actually get some sleep." With that, Lucy lay down and pulled the quilt over her head. Startled, her ghost sat unmoving and speechless. After a moment, she pulled down the quilt and looked at the ghost pointedly, "Do you mind?" she asked, nodding toward the door.

Lucy's ghost jumped up. "I'm so sorry. Of course you must rest. We can resume tomorrow."

Lucy lay down then sat right back up again.

"Your name is Harry Truman? Like the president?"

Harry Truman gave her a pained smile. "Yes, I'm afraid so."

Lucy watched as her ghost vanished and then reappeared for another moment and said, "Good night."

Sighing, she buried herself under her quilt and went to sleep.

As a soft chiming issued from the porcelain clock filled her ears, Lucy turned over, pulled the pillow over her head, and groaned. Two hours had passed in what seemed like two minutes. "What a dream," she said with a yawn, throwing her feet onto the cold hardwood floor. "Next paycheck, I'm buying a rug," she muttered as she shuffled, shivering, into the bathroom. Fifteen minutes later, she was dressed and standing in front of the kitchen sink, inhaling a quick slice of toast and cup of coffee. Turning to grab her coat and purse off the hook next to the back door, she found herself nose to nose again with her midnight visitor. Her purse and coat hit the floor with a thud as she realized that this time, she was definitely not asleep. Lucy backed against the door in terror, her heart pounding against her chest.

Her ghost friend walked toward her slowly, his transparent hands held out beseechingly. "Please, I beg of you, don't panic. I just wanted to wish you a pleasant day. If it's all right, I'll just wait here until you return." His smile was rueful and charming.

Lucy tried to compose herself. With shaking hands, she picked up her things and turned to her unwanted guest. "Mr. Truman, right? Hi. Listen, thank you for being so nice about haunting my home, but I really don't know what I can do for you, since it's clear that I am losing my mind and will most likely lose my job. So, if you're not here when I get back, well, that would be great, OK? Thanks." With that, Lucy went out, slamming the door behind her.

# TWO

All that day, Lucy fought a raging headache as she watched the chain conveyor transport packaged rolls to the shipping section of the large commercial bakery where she'd worked since graduating from high school. Every so often, she would reach out and pull aside misprinted or improperly wrapped packages that would be discounted and put out in the front outlet store for sale. *Not brain surgery*, she thought, but it was better than nothing, which was just about what everyone else in her small town was doing since the exodus of most of the town's industry to Mexico or Taiwan or wherever. At first, it had been great because Jerry worked in the same department; he was a packaging supervisor. They could eat lunch together and usually went out after work. However, lately, Jerry had been begging off going out, preferring to eat at her house and crash in front of the television.

Lucy rubbed at the spot of pain in her forehead and pulled another package off the belt. That made twelve in the last fifteen minutes. Lucy slid off her stool and pushed the button to shut down the belt. She waited as the buzzer echoed through the cavernous building, summoning Dave, the bakery's owner, and Jerry. After each had nodded solemnly at her explanation, Jerry went off to fix the problem. Lucy looked up to see Dave staring at her.

"You OK, Lucy?" he asked, "You're lookin' a little peaked." Dave was a really nice man. One of those self-made millionaires who, despite his prosperity, still drove his first car and dressed in the best Walmart had to offer. Lucy appreciated that he was so kind to her, despite the fact that she was dating Jerry, whom he did not seem to like much. Dave's aversion to Jerry was well known around the bakery and much puzzled over since Jerry was Dave's nephew.

Lucy looked into the grim but open face that frowned at her with so much concern. Dave and Jerry shared the same blond hair and watery blue eyes, but the resemblance ended there. Where Jerry was tall and lean, Dave tended to run to fat and wore a face continually flushed with the combination of hard work and high blood pressure. Lucy rubbed a spot over her right eye and smiled at him.

"I'm fine. Just had some bad dreams last night. Had a hard time sleeping," she said, hoping he wouldn't ask about Jerry.

Dave stared at her for another moment. "Go home," he said firmly. "I'll clock you at a full day. Take a sick day tomorrow if you're still feelin' poorly." He patted her shoulder and then stalked off to yell at his nephew and restart the line. Lucy smiled at Dave's retreating back. She knew that if she tried to thank him, he would just brush her off, so she sent up a prayer of thanks instead and made a silent request that whatever ailed his big, soft heart would be healed.

Picking up her stuff, Lucy went out to her latest car, a beaten-up 1980 Chevy Impala. It ran great but was missing the headliner, so at the end of every trip, Lucy had to give her hair a good shake to rid herself of the insulation that fell from the ceiling. She got in and looked up to see Jerry trotting across the parking lot toward her.

"Hey," he said, poking his head in the window. "I might not make it over tonight. Dave's got me going through all the boxes looking for more defects, so I'll be here late. What were you going to make for dinner?"

Lucy looked at him for a moment. "I hadn't thought about dinner yet," she replied. *Especially since it's only ten o'clock in the morning*, she added silently. It didn't escape her that Jerry hadn't asked how she was feeling.

"Oh well, I'll just see you tomorrow then." Jerry slapped the roof of the car and took off in a jog back to the bakery. Lucy stared at his back and started her car. The minute she left the parking lot, Jerry was forgotten as her mind turned to her new dilemma. All the way home, she wondered what she was going to find when she walked in the door. "Vampires," she mused aloud, "or a bearded giant here to tell me I'm really a wizard."

While pulling up her cracked cement driveway, Lucy studied the little white house she had inherited from her aunt. Built in the fifties, when tiny Cape Cods were all the rage among the finer postwar housing developments, it still boasted more acreage than the new Colonial homes they were building outside of town. Lucy enjoyed owning the little home, despite the work it seemed to need every spring. The recent roof repair had all but obliterated her savings.

Aside from the peeling paint that hinted of her next major expense, everything looked normal. Lucy parked in the driveway and got out. She approached the back door with caution and listened. She could hear music—blues, or jazz maybe. She couldn't tell which but knew it hadn't been on when she left. Steeling herself, she opened the back door and stepped into the kitchen. Either the music had stopped, or it had never been on in the first place. Nothing but the hum of the ancient Frigidaire greeted her. Lucy exhaled the breath she hadn't realized she had been holding. "I'm fine," she breathed. "I'm not crazy, just tired." Dropping her things on the table, she went to the sink and filled a glass with water. In the cabinet next to her, she found a bottle of painkillers and shook out enough to knock a headache out of an elephant's head. Swallowing the lot, she refilled the glass and carried it with her into the living room.

"Hello," said her ghost from the armchair in front of the record player. "I didn't realize you would be home so early. I hope you don't mind, but I took the liberty of organizing your album collection. You have a wonderful assortment of blues and jazz singers here, though, if you don't mind my saying, you must be the last person in America to still play albums."

"Funny thing, coming from someone who's been dead since the eighties," Lucy murmured, reestablishing a tight grip on the glass she had almost dropped. She moved over to the faded, plaid, wool couch and sat down before her knees could give out.

Harry chuckled. Lucy noticed that he had a pleasant laugh and a smile that crinkled his eyes at the corners. She sat and studied him as he replaced the Ella Fitzgerald she had heard earlier with Billy Holiday. He was young as if he'd died in his mid-twenties which would make him about the same age as Lucy. His hair was really more a faded red than the blond she had originally thought, but his eyes were the same sky blue, much lighter than her own, which were a darker blue. They were almost as light as Jerry's but more vivid in color, possibly because his skin looked like he'd spent a great deal of time outdoors.

*Interesting*, Lucy thought. *How many ghosts have tans?*

Harry was dressed in the same denim shirt and tan pants he'd had on earlier, but what she had thought was a plaid car coat was really a hunting jacket with little pockets for shotgun shells and a leather patch on the shoulder. Though the clothes appeared to be of good quality, they were well worn, almost threadbare in places. Looking down, she noted that the hiking boots were, in fact, Dr. Martens before they had become the trendy Doc Martens. *A ghost with bad feet*, she joked to herself.

Finished with his musical selections, Harry set aside the album cover and turned the volume down low on the stereo. Lucy watched as he took a seat next to her. "Well, now," he said. "What say you and I get acquainted first before we get down to business? Or will your shiftless, chauvinistic young man be joining us?"

Lucy looked at her visitor with surprise. "Jerry's not shiftless; he works very hard and just doesn't have the energy sometimes." Lucy stopped and wondered why she was defending Jerry when she herself thought he could help out once in a while. She shook her head to clear the jumble of thoughts and then said, "Anyway, he's not coming over. He's got to work late at the bakery." She stopped again and this time wondered why she was blathering on about Jerry when there was a figment of her imagination sitting across from her. Lucy took a deep breath and said, "Why don't you start from the beginning. I'm afraid I don't remember much of what you said last night, and I'm still not sure I haven't lost my mind."

Harry smiled. "Well, it's all depressingly simple. To begin at the end, my unfortunate demise occurred in the spring of 1985. I was traveling through Norway, trying my hand at photography. There's an amazing rock formation there, and, well...I slipped and fell into the Lysefjord."

Shocked, Lucy stared at him. "Good grief! Didn't anyone see you? Someone who could have gone for help?"

Harry shook his head. "No, no one saw, and it wouldn't have mattered anyway. I'm sure I died instantly. My body was caught under a rock formation under water, so there was nothing to indicate that I had fallen. The real trouble began with the theft of my knapsack. Everything I owned was in that bag, including my passport. If it had been turned in, my family could have surmised that I was dead. Instead, they were left to wonder, and I was doomed to this existence."

"OK," Lucy replied slowly. "So...what does that mean...'this existence'?"

Harry leaned back in the chair and looked at the ceiling. "It appears to be a type of metaphysical holding pattern. As best as I can tell, we are all being held here by our families, who wonder where we are and assume that we are still alive. Or perhaps we are holding ourselves here, needing to provide our families with some closure before we can move on—'unfinished business' or something like that."

Lucy was afraid to ask but did anyway. "Who's 'we'?"

Leaning forward, he rested his elbows on his knees. "Last night, you were awakened by voices." He paused. When Lucy nodded, he went on. "We were discussing who would approach you first. We decided that it would be best if just one of us showed ourselves. Since I found you, it was I who would be the first to make contact." Harry glanced at her for a moment and then went on. "There are quite a lot of us, actually. Some are just wandering, not quite understanding their situation, and others are perfectly content with their lot. Then there are many, like me, who have been waiting for someone living to come along who can help us contact our families."

*What happens if everyone in your family dies before they find out?* Lucy wondered.

Harry frowned. "That's where it gets a bit confusing. You see... there are some of us who have been earthbound for a very long time. It's possible that they still have someone looking for them—children, or grandchildren. Others have gone on with the deaths of their last living relatives. The ghosts who have been here the longest are content here. That's the confusing part, since it implies that it is not our families that keep us here but ourselves." Harry looked at her sheepishly. "I don't quite have it all figured out yet."

Lucy rubbed her head and said, "Why don't you just write your family a note? If you can organize my albums, you can certainly pick up a pencil and tell them, 'Hey, it's me, Harry. I'm dead. See you on the other side.'"

Harry gave her another sheepish look. "I'm afraid it's not quite that easy, as I seem to have lost track of them. You see, before I died, I suffered from wanderlust and...well...after my death, that didn't change. When I found out that I could travel anywhere in the world, I, um—." Harry paused, embarrassed. "Well, I took full advantage."

"You mean to tell me that you died, and the first thing that crossed your mind was to swim the Amazon or stroll along the Great Wall of China?" Lucy said scornfully.

"I'm afraid so." Harry looked down at his hands folded in his lap. "Time is much different for us. It's loose, fluid-like. We don't have the same sense of it passing as we did when we were living. It gets worse, though." Harry paused and looked up at Lucy. "I've only one family member left, my younger sister. She was only ten when I died. A few years ago, I thought I would see how my family was doing. Imagine my surprise to find everyone was gone."

"Gone?" Lucy asked.

"My father died when I was still alive." Harry stopped, his face pensive. Lucy watched as his features wrestled with conflicting emotions. No stranger to the pain of losing a family member, Lucy immediately felt a kinship. She sat silent for a moment, as Harry appeared lost in his family history. She spoke only when he seemed to rouse himself.

"Your dad?" Lucy prompted.

Harry looked at her quietly for a moment and then began. "My father was a physician. My mother was a teacher, and my older sister, Lillian, worked as my father's secretary. It was always assumed that I would join him after university, but after my gap year...I didn't come back." Harry's face took on a sorrowful expression. "I can't help but feel I let my father down. He was a wonderful man, would do anything for us. When my school friends would complain about their

13

dads, I had to make things up. I know I drove him to distraction with my wanderings, but he never said a word. My mother had hoped I would settle down, if only for his sake. When I left for Australia, he simply smiled and said, 'Go with God, Son.' I never knew it was killing him inside. When my mother wrote to me of his death, I was in New Zealand. I missed his funeral by a week." Harry shook his head and stared at his hands.

"What happened to your mother and your sisters?" Lucy asked.

Harry looked up at her. "From what I could gather, my mother passed away just a month after I died, and Lillian died of cancer about ten years later. I found their graves near our home. By the time I realized what I was doing and returned to my home, Anna was grown and gone. She'd be almost forty now. I haven't been able to find her or discover anything about her."

"She would've been only twenty when your sister died. Wouldn't she have been in college? Or staying with family?" Lucy asked.

"I don't know," Harry answered.

Lucy frowned. "There's a lot you don't know. I thought when you died, you suddenly knew all the secrets of the universe. Or you got to see Saint Peter at the gates of heaven and you could ask him."

Harry just looked at Lucy and shook his head. "Only our abilities to travel and communicate have changed. We need someone like you to help us."

"What do you mean, 'someone like me,' and how did you find me, anyway?" Lucy asked.

"Do you remember a Maeve O'Connell?" Harry asked.

Lucy thought for a moment. "The only O'Connell I can remember was an old woman who used to sit at the bus stop where my aunt picked me up after school." Lucy smiled at the memory. "Every day I would see her sitting there, not talking to anyone. Every day I said hello, and she would just look at me. One day, some kids were chasing on me. Mrs. O'Connell told me to sit next to her and started talking about a garden. When my aunt picked me up, I told her all about Mrs. O'Connell's garden. She just looked at me like I was crazy. After that day, I never saw Mrs. O'Connell again." Lucy shook her head. "I wonder what happened to her."

"She was dead," Harry said quietly as Lucy stared at him. "Maeve O'Connell had been a resident of a nursing home. One day she just wandered away. After you told your aunt about her, the police found her body in the backyard of an abandoned farmhouse not far from the home."

"How do you know all this? I was just a little kid at the time," Lucy asked incredulously.

"Sometimes people are with us for a very short time if they've met with an accident and have died without any family close by. Patsy, Maeve's niece, drowned while swimming off the coast of Hawaii. She told me the story before her body was found."

"Why didn't she tell you how to find me?" Lucy asked.

"Not enough time," Harry replied. "Her husband was with the search and rescue team who recovered her body a few days later."

Lucy sighed, "I guess I should be glad. I don't think a ten-year-old would've been much help to you."

"Oh no, Patsy died only two years ago. It took me this long to find you," Harry said. "But you're right—a child wouldn't have been very helpful. Most children with your ability are institutionalized or heavily medicated. That's why most of us agree not to talk to children."

"How many children have you found?" Lucy questioned.

"Almost all very young children can see us and most animals can too. My father would have said it's because babies and young children live in a state of grace, but I think it's due to the fact that they don't know that we're not supposed to exist. As they grow older, most children lose their ability to see us. Some, like you, have such strong talents in the paranormal that you never outgrow the gifts you are born with, despite what you are taught about ghosts."

"Sort of like Peter Pan," Lucy said with a weak laugh. "Didn't seem to bother him that he wasn't supposed to be able to fly."

Harry smiled. "Yes, quite."

Lucy ran a tired hand over her eyes. "What if I'm just crazy?" she asked. She dropped her hand and looked at Harry speculatively. "If you're not really here and you're just a figment of my imagination, then I'm actually talking to myself, aren't I?"

Harry shook his head. "I can assure you that you are not crazy."

"But if I were crazy, then that's exactly what my mind would tell me, right?" she countered.

Harry smiled. "Crazy people don't wonder if they're crazy...they just are."

Lucy thought about that for a second and then gave up. "All this is really interesting, but I came home because I wasn't feeling so hot. If you don't mind, I'm going to take a nap."

Concerned, Harry studied Lucy. She was pale and looked tired. Harry gave her a small smile. "I'm sorry to have tired you so. By all means, go get some rest." Lucy's ghost turned off the record player and, with a small wave, vanished.

Lucy trudged up the stairs, shedding clothes on the way to the bedroom. Clad only in her bra and panties, she crawled under the quilt and fell into a sound sleep.

# THREE

Hours later, Lucy awoke feeling refreshed. She opened her eyes to see the late afternoon sun streaming in through lace curtains that adorned the room's only window. Throwing her feet to the floor, Lucy stood and stretched, closing her eyes to savor each and every crack of her back as her vertebrae fell into place. Dropping her arms, she opened her eyes to see Harry standing just inside the door. "Jesus!" she cried, grabbing the quilt and wrapping it around her body. "Don't you ever knock?"

"So sorry." He chuckled. Harry turned his back as Lucy reached out to grab her robe from the bathroom door. Lucy tied the ratty old robe around her tightly and returned the quilt to the bed. "You can turn around now."

Harry turned and gave Lucy a charming smile. "Your shiftless young man is here," He said politely. Lucy glared at her ghost and then walked through him and out the door. Downstairs, she heard someone rummaging in her kitchen. She traveled the few steps across the living room to the kitchen door, where she stood with her arms crossed over her chest. She watched as Jerry rearranged her refrigerator, looking for something to eat. She shook her head as he took out a plastic-wrapped package of lasagna, sniffed it, and put it into the microwave. Lucy wondered why the lasagna wasn't good enough when she served it last night. Jerry turned to get a plate and noticed Lucy standing in the doorway.

"Oh...hi," he said, startled. "Dave had to run an errand, so I thought I'd stop by and see how you were feeling."

"Liar," Harry said from over her shoulder. Lucy jumped and looked quickly from Jerry to Harry.

Jerry paused in his rummaging and turned to Lucy. "Did you just say something?" he asked.

Both Lucy and Harry stared at Jerry in surpise. Lucy shook her head as Harry moved closer to the puzzled man. "Liar," Harry said again. This time, his mouth was just inches away from Jerry's ear. Jerry frowned and shook his head.

"Must be hearing things," he muttered, and then resumed his search through the cabinet.

Lucy gave her ghost a questioning look. "Don't worry," Harry said with contempt. "He can't hear or see me. Good thing, too. I would call him a liar to his face. He never made it past the refrigerator door."

Though still a novice at the paranormal business, Lucy was smart enough to know not to talk to Harry in front of Jerry, so she waved her hand at him instead. At Jerry's curious look, she murmured something about dust. Lucy gave Harry a pointed look, willing him to leave. Harry, in turn, pretended not to notice and turned to gaze at Jerry with a bland expression. Blissfully ignorant of the situation, Jerry got out a plate and fork and then turned to the fridge for a bottle of beer. Lucy looked down at the single place setting.

"Where's yours?" Harry asked, echoing her thoughts. Jerry sat in front of his plate and took a long pull from the bottle of beer. When the microwave dinged, he looked at Lucy. "I think it's ready," he said. Lucy tried not to sigh and then went to fetch his lasagna.

"He really is considerate, isn't he?" Harry said, sitting down across from the subject of his disdain. It took Lucy a moment to realize that Jerry had been speaking. "Come again?" she asked as she slid a slice of melting lasagna onto his plate and sat down in the only empty chair left.

"Aren't you listening?" Jerry frowned at Lucy as he cut into his food. Lucy watched him shovel a forkful of lasagna into his mouth and then sputter as the searing heat made contact with the tender skin on the roof of his mouth. Pouring the cold beer into his mouth to ease the pain, Jerry glared at Lucy as if it were her fault. Lucy glanced at Harry, who simply shook his head in disgust.

After dramatically checking his mouth for possible third-degree burns, Jerry took another long drink and then pushed the offending lasagna away. "I don't have much time," he said petulantly.

"Pity," Harry interrupted. Lucy glared at him.

"I just thought I'd make sure you're OK," Jerry continued.

"Uh-huh," Harry said, interrupting again. Lucy glared at him again.

Jerry sat and looked at Lucy as she gave the back door a dirty look.

"What is he waiting for, a medal?" Harry remarked.

"Dave's going to be back at the bakery soon, so I'd better get going." Jerry got up and took another beer from the fridge.

"Bye-bye," Harry called to him. Lucy just sat and said nothing.

At the door, Jerry turned and looked at Lucy hesitantly. "If I have a chance, I'll come back later," he said. Lucy smiled and gave him a small wave. Puzzled, Jerry closed the door behind him.

Lucy turned to Harry, who sat and looked at the closed door while absentmindedly drumming his fingers on the table.

"Now what?" she asked the pensive ghost.

"There's something not quite right about him," Harry said, still staring at the door.

Lucy ignored the comment and pushed herself up from the table. Harry looked after her as she left the kitchen. "Where are you going?" he asked.

"To get dressed," she called out as she went up to her room, "We're going to the library."

Harry shrugged and then went back to staring at the door.

An hour later, Harry sat quietly as Lucy drove the short distance to the town's only library. Like most small Midwestern towns, Paris was little more than a cluster of turn-of-the-century buildings that surrounded a small, grassy town square. The blackened windows of deserted storefronts dotted the business district like missing teeth. The few shops that remained vied for the scant business that the bank and the medical arts building brought in. For a brief time, Marty's Kard Kart enjoyed a huge surge in sales during the Beanie Babies frenzy, until everyone, from the tailor to the barber, started selling the ubiquitous children's toys. Now the big red heart in Kard Kart's window hung askew, and dust powdered the fading flamingoes and pelicans that remained in the window. An equally faded Silly Bandz sign hung next to the drooping heart with a somewhat fresh Rainbow Loom sign next to it. Lucy slowed the car to peer in the window of Paris's only clothing store to see Miss Alice, her late aunt's friend, waving cheerfully, a duster in her hand. The store did so little business that during high school, Lucy's job had been to dust the clothes. Lucy waved back, stifling a laugh as Harry also waved enthusiastically.

22

Main Street ended just past the VFW, where it became an obscure rural route that ran through vast fields devoted to small-scale agriculture. This particular part of the state was flat and featureless and was given to monochromatic seasons. At one time, there had been several large factories that took advantage of the town's cheap land and close proximity to Interstate 70. However, during the mideighties, both the plastics plant and the auto parts factory had relocated to Mexico, leaving much of Paris's population in the dust. Those who could retired, and the rest made the hour commute to Columbus to find work. All that remained were the bakery, where Lucy was employed, and the Ohio State Farming Cooperative. Like most other small towns in Ohio, Paris's city council spent most of its time attempting to lure other types of industry, without luck.

Lucy drove the short distance across town in just under ten minutes, arriving at the small brick box that housed the library.

"What are we doing here?" Harry asked as Lucy parked in the empty parking lot.

Lucy turned off the car and threw her keys into her purse. "We're going to use the library's computer to find your family," she explained. Harry followed Lucy out of the car and up the steps. Inside, Lucy gave the library's only occupant, an elderly librarian, an affectionate hello and then headed for the table that held the library's only two computers. "The library has access to the Internet," she whispered as they settled in front of the terminal. "It's our best bet to find your family."

"I'm not very familiar with this Internet," Harry whispered back.

"Why are you whispering?" Lucy asked.

"Why are you?" Harry shot back. "I seriously doubt that your octogenarian bibliophile can hear a thing. How are you using the Internet?"

Lucy glared at Harry as she logged on. "The Internet's like this huge electronic universe of information. If you can't find it on the Internet, it doesn't exist." Harry watched in amazement as Lucy's fingers flew over the keys. She searched for the site she was looking for.

"You're quite good at this," he remarked, impressed. Lucy glanced at him and turned back to the screen.

"I took some classes at the community college in Springfield, hoping I could find a better-paying job. I come here a lot to practice—not that it's done me any good," she explained. "Unfortunately, someone has to die here before another job opens up." Lucy made a face at Harry's expression. "No offense," she said.

"None taken," he replied, sitting back.

Lucy paused with her fingers still on the keys. "How do you not know about the Internet? If you can go anywhere, you should have seen someone in front of a computer by now."

Harry shrugged. "I don't know. I've spent much of my time, as it is, in places where the culture is more open to the metaphysical. I've not really paid attention to technology. I can recall when computers were available for use in one's home, but not much else."

Lucy regarded him a moment longer. "When did you say you died?"

"1986."

"That was more than twenty-five years ago," Lucy answered. "How did you lose so many years?"

"I guess I've been traveling so much that I didn't really keep track," he answered. "Like I said before, time is different for us."

After a few more moments, Lucy found the site she was looking for. "Here we go." She turned to Harry as he peered at the screen. "This site is a type of electronic telephone book...an international white pages." Looking back at the screen, she began to type. "Now, we're looking for...." Lucy glanced at Harry.

"Oh," Harry said, leaning toward the screen, "Anna Truman, T-R-U-M-A-N. Like the president."

Lucy entered the name as Harry checked her spelling. "Now, I'll ask it to search all of the United Kingdom in case she's wandered as far as you have."

"How long will this take?" Harry asked, amazed.

"It's done," Lucy said, peering at the screen. "It looks like it found a few Anna Trumans: one in London, one in Wales, and others in...other places. It looks like the one in London has e-mail." Lucy looked over at Harry, who was staring at the screen. "What should I write? I can't tell her I'm sitting next to her dead brother."

Harry glanced at her and shrugged. "Perhaps you could just inquire if she has a brother...in general. Say you're an old school mate or something."

Lucy gave that a thought and then shrugged and typed out the message. It was only a few moments before they received a response.

"She must be online," she remarked as she read the short note.

"On line for what?" Harry asked.

"Online...not on line. 'Online' means she's using her computer right now. Too bad we don't have instant messaging." Lucy shook her head. "No, no brother." She sat back and looked at Harry, who was still staring at the computer screen. "Well, I guess we could call the one in Wales," she said hesitantly. "How much is a call to Wales, anyway?"

Harry pointed to the screen. "Could you go back to that phone book? Some of them had ages and middle initials."

Lucy clicked the "back" button and brought up the list. Harry glanced at it and then disappeared for a moment. When he returned, he was shaking his head. "No, none of them are her."

Lucy felt bad for him. "Don't worry; there are other ways of searching," she reassured him, turning back to the computer. "I'll try some of the other search engines."

Lucy and Harry spent the rest of the afternoon in front of the terminal, without success. Harry sat dejected as she logged off. Turning to her ghost friend, Lucy spoke quietly. "I'm sorry, Harry, but I wouldn't give up just yet. There's a locator service we use. They do searches all the time. I would've tried them first, but they can cost a lot of money, and I was hoping we would find your sister on our own."

Harry gave her a small smile. "Please don't think me ungrateful. You've done far more than I have a right to expect." Harry fell silent as the librarian approached. Patting Lucy's shoulder with obvious affection, she sadly informed them that the library was closing. Lucy stood quickly and hugged her. Harry smiled at Lucy's affection for the elderly woman. After a brief chat between the two women, Harry and Lucy left the library.

Neither spoke on the ride back to the house. As Lucy pulled up the driveway and parked, Harry cleared his throat. Lucy shut off the car and looked at him curiously. "I want to thank you for your efforts on my behalf," he said slowly, and stopped.

"What's wrong?" Lucy asked as she got out of the car and shook out her hair.

Harry appeared across from her the roof of the car across from them. "There's something I haven't told you yet," he said. Lucy just looked at him. Taking a deep breath, Harry continued. "There are others who are going to want your help."

Lucy stared at him. "Others? What others?" she demanded. Suddenly conscious of how exposed Lucy was, Harry looked around the small yard and spied Mrs. Kelly, her next-door neighbor, watching Lucy. As he began ushering her toward the house, Lucy also realized how she must look standing in her backyard, yelling at herself. Quickly she headed for the back door, with Harry following. Fumbling, she managed to unlock her door. Stepping into the kitchen, she stopped so suddenly that Harry walked right through her. They both stopped at the sight of the small kitchen filled with people. Most were just milling around, while some sat at Lucy's table. One gentleman passed the time rearranging her pantry. All turned and looked up expectantly as Lucy and Harry walked in.

An attractive young woman dressed in a bikini top and cutoff shorts walked up to Harry and folded her arms across her chest. "Well?" she asked. Harry turned and ushered Lucy into the kitchen, leaving the door to swing closed behind them. Placing himself protectively in front of Lucy, Harry shook his head at the group.

"We had an agreement," he said angrily. "You were to wait until I called on you."

The young beachgoer tossed her garishly blond hair and rolled her large, liquid-brown eyes. "Whatever, Mister President," she drawled. "Did she find anything?"

Annoyed, Lucy pushed through Harry and addressed the opaque young woman. "First of all, if you've got something to say, you say it to me. Second, I don't appreciate you barging into my home like this. You might be dead, but that doesn't give you a right to trespass. Third...well I don't have a third, so...you all can just leave." Lucy walked through several more ghosts to the living room. Harry watched her stop in the doorway to the living room.

"Good grief!" she cried as she spied the ghosts crammed wall to wall, some standing inside others to make room. Harry followed her as she brushed the specters aside and made her way to the crowded stairwell. Upstairs, ghosts filled the hallway and bedroom. The only unoccupied room was the small closet that had been converted into a bathroom. Lucy went in, slamming the door as Harry walked through. She turned and glared at him.

"So how many are there? Hmm?" she asked, her voice tense with anger. "And what do you expect me to do? Quit my job and dedicate my life to sending you guys on to the great beyond? I don't mind helping you, and maybe a couple of others, but this is ridiculous."

Harry stood silently, watching Lucy pace the length of the tiny room. Exhausted, she sat on the toilet seat and dropped her head into her hands.

"I can't believe this," she muttered. "I *am* losing my mind."

Harry kneeled in front of her and looked up into her face. "I'm sorry, Lucy," he said, "I told them it wasn't fair to expect you to help everyone. You must understand, though, that they are desperate to leave this existence. And for the first time in a very long while, they have a way to do so. You can't fault them for trying." Harry held out his hands beseechingly. "I can't ask you to help them, but I hope you will consider it."

Lucy glared at him for a moment and then closed her eyes. "They're not going away until I help them, are they?"

Harry paused and shook his head.

Lucy sat back, deflated. "Could you give me a moment alone, please?"

Harry stood. "Of course, you will want some time to think all this over."

Lucy stood and sighed, "No, I have to use the facilities." Harry gave an embarrassed smile and vanished through the door. She could hear him ushering out the ghosts that loitered in her bedroom. Lucy shook her head as she turned to the mirror over the sink. Pulling her thick blond hair back into a loose bun, Lucy bathed her face and neck with a bracing splash of water, unable to relish the tingle it brought to her skin. Patting dry, she went out into the bedroom and was relieved to find it empty. Lucy lay across the bed and closed her eyes. Another headache was on the horizon. Lucy groaned when she realized that the aspirin were in the kitchen. Unwilling to face her newest houseguests, Lucy pulled her pillow over her head and willed herself to sleep.

# FOUR

It was dark outside when Lucy awoke to a gentle murmuring. Reluctantly, she opened her eyes to see Harry's face very close to hers as he quietly whispered her name. Feigning fatigue, Lucy rolled over and buried her head under the pillow again. Harry's voice grew insistent.

"What?" Lucy moaned, her voice muffled by the pillow.

"He's back," Harry said urgently.

"Who's back?" she grumbled, even though she knew damn well who he was talking about.

"Your gentleman friend," Harry replied.

Lucy crawled out from under the pillow in time to see the door opening behind Harry. Jerry stepped into the room and glared at her. "I told you I was coming back," he whined.

Lucy groaned as she rolled her aching body off the bed. "Your point?" she asked as she picked up her robe and stepped into the bathroom. Slamming the door on Jerry's reply, she took her time as she peeled off the jeans and T-shirt she had been wearing earlier and pulled on the robe. She slowly rinsed the sour taste in her mouth with industrial-strength mouthwash and then reluctantly exited her sanctuary. Jerry unknowingly sat next to Harry on the bed, still haranguing her as if she had never left the room. Nodding without listening to his comments, Lucy walked past him and left the bedroom.

The house was surprisingly empty as she made her way down to the kitchen, with Jerry following on her heels. She entered the kitchen, only mildly startled to see Harry already sitting at the table, waiting. Going to the refrigerator, Lucy pulled out orange juice and poured a huge glass. Jerry stared at her as she drank greedily and then slammed the glass down with a cough. Lucy walked past him to fetch the bottle of painkillers. With a smaller refill of orange juice, she sat down at the table and shook out three of the extra-strength pills. Ignoring Harry's questioning look, Lucy washed down the pills and swallowed a fourth for good measure. She watched as Jerry slowly sat in the seat before her, forcing Harry to move to the remaining chair.

"I told you I was coming back," Jerry whined again. Lucy gave him a baleful stare. She sat, torn between resenting him and wanting to please him. The feelings of resentment were new to her. She turned and glared at Harry, aware that he was at least partly responsible for her change of heart. Jerry sat alarmed as she gave the back door another dirty look. Harry simply shrugged and smiled at her pleasantly.

"I suppose you want something to eat," she sighed. Jerry smiled, relieved that Lucy seemed to be returning to normal.

"That'd be great," he said brightly, and then soured, remembering he was supposed to be angry with her. "You know, I expected you to be awake when I got here," Jerry said crisply. Harry snorted but said nothing as Lucy glared at him again. Getting up, she opened the freezer and took out a rock-hard container of beef stew. As it defrosted in the microwave, she sat down at the table and sliced a loaf of Italian bread. Jerry talked as she buttered and seasoned each slice before placing it in the oven. The room began to fill with the smell of garlic and butter. Lucy feigned interest as Jerry droned on and on about the bakery.

"It took me the whole day, but I managed to find the shipment with all the defective packages. Dave wanted to recycle them, but I called and reamed the supplier. Got a credit for the whole batch, even though it was just the one box that was bad." Jerry sat puffed up with self-importance. "Dave's pissed at me. Thinks I'm cheating the suppliers. He just doesn't have good business sense."

*That's why he's a millionaire and you're not*, Lucy countered mentally as she pulled the thawed beef stew out of the microwave and set it to simmer on the stove. Harry, for once, sat silently, thoughtfully watching the other man. She said nothing as Jerry continued to bad-mouth his uncle. Pulling out dishes, Lucy set the table for dinner. It wasn't until she sat down that she realized she had set a place for Harry. Jerry stopped in midsentence and stared at the extra place setting.

"What's going on, Luce?" Jerry asked. Lucy glanced at Harry, who sat frowning at the plate before him.

Lucy stared at Jerry for a moment, unable to think. Next to her, Harry spoke quietly, "Tell him a guest is coming."

Lucy smiled brightly. "While I was at the library today, I spoke with Mrs. Myers. She mentioned she might be stopping by...so...I wanted to have a place set for her in case she comes in time for dinner."

"Doubt that old hag will even remember talking to you," Jerry snorted. Lucy winced at the hateful reference to her beloved friend as she got up to fetch the fragrant stew and bread. Jerry inhaled the food without a word as Lucy sat and desultorily stirred the brown broth. Jerry continued his boss-bashing monologue, pausing only to shovel more food into his mouth. Talking through the food in his mouth, Jerry became so involved in his ego masturbation that small bits of food fell out as he spoke. Lucy and Harry watched in disgust as a spray of beef and bread crumbs spattered the table. Jerry took no notice as Lucy pushed away her bowl of stew, now dotted with spittle. Harry continued to stare at the other man, his face unreadable. Using a slice of bread to mop up the remnants of his meal, Jerry shoved the lot into his mouth and settled back, letting out a satisfied belch.

"Well," he said, belching again. "I've got to get home. I told Dave I'd be in early." Jerry got up from the table and gave her a quick peck on the top of her head. After raiding the refrigerator for the last of her beer, Jerry opened the back door. As an afterthought, he turned and asked, "So, you feelin' better?" Before she could answer, though, Jerry replied with an enthusiastic "Great!" then slammed the door behind him. Harry and Lucy sat and stared at each other for a moment before Harry shook his head in disgust.

"Don't tell me you actually love that dolt?" he asked, incredulous.

Lucy sighed as she got up to clean up the dirty dishes. "He wasn't like this when we first started dating," she replied as she scrubbed a pot at the sink. "Jerry was much more attentive in the beginning. He would take me out to dinner or to the movies." Lucy paused in her meditations. "I guess I was a little star-struck," she admitted as she cast an embarrassed glance at Harry. "I had a crush on Jerry in high school." She smiled ruefully as Harry suppressed a chuckle. "I know it sounds stupid, but Jerry was really popular then. I was just a skinny, geeky freshman when he first said hi to me." She looked out the window at nothing and then with a soapy finger, tucked an errant strand of hair behind her ear. "You have to understand that I was worse than a wallflower in high school; I was wallpaper. He was a junior and a starter for the varsity basketball team. All through high school, I fantasized about him."

Lucy turned away from the sink to wash the counter and table, still too embarrassed to look at Harry. "When I started working at the bakery, I kind of hoped he would ask me out, even though he'd just broken up with my friend, Mary Beth. I couldn't believe it when he actually did." Lucy stared around the small kitchen at a loss for something else to clean. Giving up, she sat down at the table. "I guess I've only got myself to blame." She shrugged. "I'd painted such a wonderful picture of Jerry in my mind that I wasn't prepared for the reality. Maybe I was hoping to capture what some of the popular kids had." Lucy swiped at the table with the cloth she still held. "Anyhow, here I am. Jerry's OK, not the greatest, but OK...and it's not like there's a whole lot of eligible bachelors in this town."

She looked up to see Harry studying her thoughtfully. "What?" she asked defensively.

Harry sat up, startled out of his musings. During Jerry's visit, Harry had seemed preoccupied. "Nothing," he replied. "I was just thinking how remarkable it is that your Jerry never noticed how little you spoke tonight." Lucy simply shrugged in answer. "Well, he is of no consequence," Harry continued, dismissing the subject. "We have a more important matter at hand."

"What's that?" Lucy asked, eyeing Harry narrowly.

Harry stood and paced the small kitchen. "We need to somehow organize the numbers of spirits who are seeking your help." Lucy started to protest but quieted at Harry's questioning glance. "I know you're not looking forward to this, but I'm sure I can make this easier for you. If we can chart the name, last address, and known family of each ghost, it may facilitate the process of notifying their families." Harry paused in his pacing. "We also need to figure out how we're going to tell them. We can't have you just dropping a bomb like that on some unsuspecting mother. We need to draft a script for you."

Lucy nodded in agreement but suddenly found she was too tired to speculate on anything more than whether or not she had any clean pajamas. As if reading her mind, Harry sat before her and reached for her hand. The movement startled Lucy, who jerked back as if burned. Harry stammered, apologizing profusely. Embarrassed by her reaction, she brushed off his apologies, claiming fatigue.

"You're absolutely right, Lucy. I've imposed on you far too much. I'll just go and see about putting together some kind of list for you." Harry gave Lucy a small smile. "I'm sorry about all this." Lucy looked into her opaque friend's face and smiled in return. Harry seemed reassured by the smile. Leaning over, his smile faded as his expression sobered. "You're doing a good thing, Lucy. Without you, these people have no hope of moving on. If it ever gets to be too much, let me know, and I'll make it stop."

Lucy laughed at the serious young man. "You'd do that for me?" she asked, amused.

Harry smiled in return. "In a minute," he replied. "Now go get some rest. I'll try and keep the spooks out."

Taking the aspirins with her, Lucy bid her ghost good-night and went up to her bedroom. Peeking around the corner, she was relieved to see the small room empty of transparent people. Lucy stripped down to her birthday suit and hopped into the shower. A quick soap and rinse left her feeling refreshed, despite the dull throb behind her eyes. After drying off, Lucy swallowed some of the aspirin then, clad in a clean T-shirt and boxer shorts, reset her alarm and climbed into bed. Even though Dave had said she could take tomorrow off, Lucy didn't want to take advantage of his generosity. Besides, she was feeling better and, barring any more supernatural visitors, she should be in good shape by tomorrow morning. Lucy closed her eyes and willed herself to relax. An image of Harry reaching for her hand came unbidden to her mind. Feeling slightly guilty, she shook the image out of her head. *It won't do any good to start digging a dead guy,* she thought, groaning at her own pun. Pulling the careworn quilt over her head, she fell asleep.

# FIVE

Lucy awoke minutes before the clock was set to chime, feeling marginally better than she had the morning before. Odd dreams had plagued her during the night, leaving her feeling disoriented, though rested. She grabbed the small clock, anticipating the alarm, and then reluctantly rolled out of the bed, shivering as her feet touched the cold hardwood floor. "Next paycheck I'm buying a rug," she mumbled. Lucy threw on her baker's whites and headed down to the kitchen for a quick cup of coffee. She was surprised and a little disappointed to see it occupied with nothing more than the aroma of the brewing automatic coffee maker. Shaking her head at her silliness, she gulped down the life-sustaining beverage and then headed off to work.

In the car, Lucy surprised herself by singing along to the radio, something she hadn't done in a long time. She was in a good mood, despite the dull pressure behind her eyes that threatened to explode into a full-blown migraine. Anticipating the headache, Lucy had thrown the entire bottle of painkillers into her bag before leaving the house. She retrieved the large plastic bottle and shook out a couple of pills as she drove. With a grimace, she swallowed them dry, coughing at the bitter powder taste. Ignoring the lingering pain, Lucy drove the short distance to the bakery in a good humor.

After parking and locking her ancient car, Lucy passed Dave on the way to the locker room to drop off her purse. Stifling his surprise, Dave merely grunted at Lucy and patted her on her shoulder. Lucy started to thank him for sending her home the day before but was waved away by the gruff yet kindly man. She wasn't surprised to see that he had already clocked her in for the day, and for an hour earlier than she usually started. Lucy shook her head and smiled, knowing already that she would clock out an hour before she actually left.

On the line, Lucy sat and stared at the endless parade of shining packages of hamburger buns. Unlike the day before, none of the packages were defective, and Lucy found her mind going numb, even as she maintained her vigil. She yawned hugely and then startled at the sight of a pair of knees traveling past her. Looking up, she saw Harry perched atop the conveyor belt, using a bag of buns for a cushion. Lucy laughed aloud and then looked around, suddenly self-conscious. Twenty feet away, Mary Beth, the line runner and her former friend, looked at her oddly but then continued working. Turning back to the belt, Lucy laughed again to see Harry hovering over the conveyor belt, bumping comically as each package passed beneath him.

"You look like you're feeling better," Harry said, his voice jumping with each bump. Lucy stifled another chuckle.

"I am now," she whispered, glancing at her former friend's retreating back. "It can get incredibly boring on the line." Lucy turned back to see Harry walking along as the conveyor belt passed beneath him in the opposite direction. He smiled as she laughed aloud.

"I used to love to climb escalators that were going the other way, didn't you?" he asked. Lucy stifled another chuckle as he floated to the floor. Harry perched next to her on an imaginary stool and watched the endless parade of packages. "Not very exciting, is it?" he asked solemnly.

"No, not really. But it pays the bills," she replied. Together they sat and watched the rolls go by. After a moment, she glanced over at Harry, who stared at the conveyor belt, his eyes wide. "Hypnotic, isn't it?" she said with a laugh. Dazed, Harry shook his head and laughed with her.

"Yes, it is," he replied. "Anyhow, I came not to distract you from your duties but to let you know that I've put together a list for us to start working on."

"Great," Lucy replied, her voice dripping with sarcasm. "I can't wait."

Chagrined, Harry gave her a small smile. "I guess it can wait. How much longer do you have here?"

Lucy sighed and glanced at her watch. "I've got another two hours before my shift ends. Why? What did you have in mind?"

"Shhh," Harry said, putting his fingers to his lips. Lucy looked at him oddly. She jumped at the touch of a hand on her shoulder. Turning, she found Dave standing behind her, a look of concern on his face.

"Everythin' all right?" he asked. "You were talkin' to yerself."

Lucy gave a nervous laugh. "I'm fine...just babbling to pass the time."

Dave looked closely at her, causing her to squirm under his scrutiny. Lucy began to wonder if Dave was angry with her. After what seemed like a long time, Dave asked quietly, "You wanna go work in the shop for a while? Louis is out on disability, so I've only got Hannah out there, and she's gonna need some help. That'll give you a break from the line."

Lucy stared at Dave in astonishment. The outlet shop located at the entrance of the large building that housed the bakery was a highly coveted job. Not only did it pay better; it was a lot more fun. The bakery-shop employees were not only in charge of the store but also gave tours to school kids. It was busy but had the advantage of being in an airy, open room rather the cavernous, windowless warehouse where the baking took place. Hannah and Louis, who staffed the shop, had been with Dave for almost thirty years each. Louis worked there because he had injured his arm in one of the giant mixers. Hannah got to work there as a sort of reward after her many years of loyal service to the bakery. For Dave to offer the job, even temporarily, to Lucy was unprecedented. She had no choice but to refuse.

"There are a lot of others who should be out there, Dave. I'll be all right here," Lucy said, shaking her head. Over Dave's shoulder, she could see Mary Beth staring at her oddly. Lucy gave her a pointed look, to which Mary Beth rolled her eyes and then walked away, shaking her head. Dave watched Mary Beth go, and then he looked back at Lucy.

"Go ahead, Lucy," Dave said with a note of finality. "Jerry can come down and cover your spot till the end of your shift." With a final pat to her shoulder, Dave shut down the line and then stalked off to find Jerry. Lucy hurried to get her things together as Harry doubled over, laughing.

"Imagine what your beau will say when he finds out he's been demoted," he said through the tears.

Lucy shot Harry a dirty look as she rushed out to avoid a confrontation with Jerry. She knew Jerry would blame her for Dave's generosity and did not want to stick around for the inevitable tantrum. Harry followed as she made her way to the locker room to change into a T-shirt. Hannah and Louis wore red smocks rather than the baker's whites that were required for the rest of the bakery. She shoved her white tunic into the locker and slammed the door. Harry continued to follow as she made her way to the front of the bakery, where the outlet store was located. Her eyes strained to adjust to the sudden burst of light as she stepped into the sunlit room. It took a moment of squinting before Lucy located the room's only occupant. Hannah's tightly permed, graying head was bent over the store's register drawer as she broke open rolls of change for the various compartments. Lucy politely cleared her throat before she entered the room. Hannah jumped, her head popping up and twisting about like a curious bird. At the sight of Lucy, she smiled broadly and waved the young woman over. Lucy went up to the counter, with Harry close behind her.

"Hello, hello!" Hannah spoke brightly. "Dave told me you were going to be helping me out while Louis is gone. I'm just getting the drawer ready before I open the doors." Turning, the older woman opened a cabinet behind her and disappeared into its depths, presenting her generous backside to Lucy and Harry. Harry politely turned away as Hannah's polyester-clad derrière swayed back and forth. "Here it is!" she cried, holding up a neatly pressed smock identical to her own. "When Dave told me you'd be coming up, I went through my closets and found my old vest. I'm pretty sure it'll fit you." Hannah leaned over and smiled into Lucy's face, saying, "I was almost as skinny as you way back when," she whispered. She gave a broad wink. "Now you just put that on, and I'll show you what needs to get done before you leave me for the day."

Lucy pulled the crisp smock over her head, inhaling the fragrant combination of fabric softener and spray starch. Harry perched on the counter, a wide smile on his face as Hannah hurried around the counter and ushered Lucy to the front of the store. Sun streamed into the store through wide floor-to-ceiling windows, warming the chilly air that kept the packages of bread and rolls fresh. In a flat box on the floor lay large plastic window decals announcing "Freshly Baked" and "Sale." Hannah dragged a small stepladder over to the first windowpane.

"Dave ordered these wonderful stickers for the windows. Remember Colorforms, those plastic pieces that would stick without any glue? Well, these are just the same thing, can you imagine? And so big! But with my big butt and Louis's bad arm, they've been sitting here for just the longest time. Jerry was supposed to do them, but I'm not sure he even tried. It would be just wonderful if you could put them up. Would that be OK?"

"Sure," Lucy replied. "Any particular order?"

"Oh, Lucy, honey," Hannah said with a smile, "whatever you think looks nice." After patting Lucy on the arm, Hannah returned to the register.

"What a lovely woman," Harry said from the top of the stepladder. Lucy smiled and nodded as she bent to the reach into carton at her feet. There were six decals large enough to cover an entire window. Lucy looked around at the twelve empty windowpanes that surrounded the room. Picking up the top decal and the stepladder, she walked over to the first set of windows, leaving Harry to hover. After a moment's consideration, Lucy decided to alternate the window decals. At the second window, she climbed to the top of the stepladder and pressed the decal to the glass. As she worked her way down the window, Lucy found herself covered by the top of the decal that had floated gently over her head. Ignoring Harry's laughter, she again started at the top of the window and again found herself fighting to keep the decal from smothering her. Harry shed ghostly tears as he rolled on the floor, convulsing with laughter. Lucy quietly cleared her throat and gave him a pointed look, nodding at the ceiling.

"Oh, all right, don't get yer knickers in a twist," he said, wiping tears from his eyes. With no noticeable effort, he floated to the ceiling as Lucy yet again climbed the stepladder. Harry smiled and continued to chuckle as he held the decal to the glass. Lucy worked her way down, smoothing the large plastic "Sale" sign like wallpaper. Back on the floor, she slowly nodded to Harry. Both of them let go of the decal on the third nod. This time, it stuck fast. Lucy smiled broadly and then nodded at the box. With Harry's help, they made quick work of the remaining decals. Finished, they stepped back and looked around the store. The brightly colored signs turned the streaming sunlight into a rainbow of colors that decorated the white tile floor like a child's finger painting.

Hannah walked up to Lucy and patted her arm. "Well, isn't that just the prettiest thing?" she exclaimed. "And it didn't take any time at all! Wait till I tell Dave how quickly you finished! He'll think Louis and I are just sitting around like a bunch of lazybones!" As if on cue, Dave opened the rear door and stepped in. A petulant Jerry followed behind him.

"Look at this!" Hannah squealed, spinning Lucy around. "Look at what a wonderful job Lucy did!" Dave smiled at Hannah indulgently as Jerry scowled over Dave's shoulder.

"Well, that looks just fine, Lucy," Dave said. "I'm mighty impressed. Jerry here couldn't even get the darn things to stay up." Behind her, Lucy heard Harry snicker as Jerry glowered at the back of Dave's head before shooting daggers at her. Lucy kept her mouth shut and smiled sweetly.

Looking at his watch, Dave turned around in time to see Jerry's scowl. "Lucy's shift is over, so I want you to stay out here with Hannah till the store closes." Jerry moved to object, but his uncle cut him off. "Lucy, I'll want you back here tomorrow morning, so you'll need to go home and get some rest. I'm switching your shift to the store's hours, so you'll need to be here by nine to help Hannah open."

Jerry made a second effort to object, but Dave had already left the room. Looking back, he glared at Lucy. "What did you say to him?" he asked, his face a mask of belligerence. Lucy opened her mouth to answer, but Jerry cut her off. "I can't believe you," Jerry growled as he advanced on the two women. "Not only did you get me stuck on the line; you got me pulling a double shift!"

Lucy moved to reply but was stopped as Hannah stepped in front of her. "Now, listen here, you little pissant," she hissed. "You're getting exactly what you deserve, so you just leave Lucy alone. Now get your sorry ass over there and unpack those rolls, and stay away from the register. I don't need your sticky fingers screwing up my tally tonight."

Shocked, Lucy and Harry stared open-mouthed at the older woman as she waved her finger in Jerry's face. Harry beamed as the now-quiet Jerry slunk off to fetch Louis's smock. Custom-made for the three-hundred-pound Louis, it hung on Jerry's thin frame like a circus tent. Hannah turned back to Lucy, shaking her head. She gave Lucy a reassuring smile as she led her to the rear of the store and out of Jerry's hearing range.

"What a *lovely* woman," Harry repeated as he followed the women.

Hannah patted Lucy's hand and looked up into the younger woman's face. "You just ignore him, sweetheart. The poor boy doesn't know his ass from a hole in the ground and thinks we can't tell. You just go on home now, and I'll see you in the morning." Lucy started to hand the smock back to her, but the kind woman stopped her. "No, no," Hannah said brightly. "That's yours now. You just keep it."

"Are you sure?" Lucy asked.

"Oh, honey, of course. It'll never fit me again," she said with a rueful smile. "In fact, you'd have to cut me half just to get it on! Now go home. I expect you here tomorrow bright and not so early!" Hannah laughed at her own joke and then went off to supervise her reluctant assistant.

Lucy and Harry beat a hasty retreat before Jerry could attempt another verbal attack. At the door, Lucy turned to see Jerry staring venomously at her. She gave him a nervous smile, and then she darted out the door after Harry.

# SIX

During the short car ride home, Jerry was soon forgotten as Harry entertained Lucy with silly versions of the songs that came on the radio. Her enjoyment soured though when they pulled up the drive. Like the day before, Lucy's home was filled with so many eager specters that they spilled out of the house and onto the lawn. She gave a dramatic sigh but said nothing as Harry groaned and shook his head.

"If you're up to it, I thought we could start working down the list," Harry said as they climbed out of the car and reluctantly approached the house.

"Fine," Lucy replied with a sigh, still amazed at the situation she now found herself in and still somewhat concerned about her mental state. At the door, she found the ghosts treating her with more deference than they'd shown the day before. Even the lovely beach girl who previously had been so rude approached with a reluctant "Hello." Harry nodded in approval as the group parted to allow Lucy through the house. She was further impressed to see her bedroom empty, allowing her the privacy to wash her face and change out of her uniform into a worn but clean T-shirt and faded, flannel-soft jeans.

Returning to the kitchen, she found Harry at the table, surrounded by ghosts and papers, a sandwich, and an icy bottle of soda set before the chair to his right. The older man who had been searching her pantry the day before gave her a gracious smile as he snapped a paper napkin across the seat with a grand gesture. Lucy gave him a small smile in return as she sat before the simple meal. Her incorporeal waiter laid the napkin across her lap and then stood to one side as she picked up the thick sandwich. Harry watched the performance with one eyebrow raised. Lucy shrugged at his expression and then bit into the most delicious turkey sandwich she'd ever eaten. Groaning in instant enjoyment, she took another bite, rolling her eyes in ecstasy at the beaming gentleman.

"This is absolutely the best sandwich I have ever had," she said between bites. She took a long pull from the soda and then moaned again. "Oh, even the soda tastes better!" Harry smiled indulgently as Lucy devoured the rest of the sandwich. Finished, she sat back in her chair with a moan of pure satisfaction.

"Lucy, meet George," Harry said as the older man took a bow. "George owned a deli in New Jersey before meeting with an unfortunate end at the hands of an irate husband." George gave Lucy a sheepish look, a lock of bright white hair falling over his sparkling blue eyes.

"She told me she was divorced," he said in a deep baritone that belied his cherubic features. "So you like my food?" he asked, a leer curling his rosebud of a mouth.

"Oh yes!" Lucy exclaimed. "That was delicious. What was in it, anyway?"

"Oh, just a little smoked turkey, some bacon, a dab of cranberry sauce," George replied. Then he leaned over and said with a dramatic whisper, "And a little magic." He wiggled his chubby fingers at Lucy, who laughed in response.

"I believe it," she sighed. George gave an appreciative chuckle as he picked up the empty plate and soda bottle. Lucy smiled her thanks and then turned to Harry, who sat shaking his head.

"Don't get too used to that; George is pretty high on the list," he warned as George shrugged. "Now to business. I've listed our ghosts by date of disappearance, thinking that it would be easier to contact families who have lost someone recently." He slid the top sheet across to Lucy, who reluctantly picked it up. "Each name has the date and circumstances of death, last known family and their address, distinguishing characteristics of the deceased for purposes of identification, and a short message for their family."

"How many are we talking about?" Lucy asked reluctantly.

"About fifty or so," Harry answered.

"That's not bad," Lucy said, nodding.

"On the first page," Harry said, "There's over two hundred in all." Lucy groaned. The other ghosts in the room shifted uncomfortably. Some mumbled words of encouragement, and others indicated concern that she might change her mind. Most said nothing but looked worried. Lucy looked around the group, seeing myriad expressions that painted their opaque faces. No matter what they appeared to be thinking, they all looked hopeful and desperate at the same time. She knew then that she couldn't let them down. With a reassuring smile, she picked up the first sheet of names and accepted the phone from Beach Girl.

"Who is Shelly Martini?" Lucy asked, looking around the room. Beach Girl raised her hand. Lucy smiled at her and then glanced back at the list. Suddenly puzzled, she looked at the piece of paper more closely. "What is this name that's right next to Shelly's?" she asked.

"That's Jeannie Allen," Harry replied. "She and Shelly were together when they disappeared."

Beach Girl spoke up as another ghost, a lovely long-haired brunette also in beachwear, appeared next to her. "Jeannie and I were driving to Florida for Spring Break when our car broke down. Two yokels picked us up in North Carolina and said they could take us the rest of the way. Bad idea," she intoned as Jeannie nodded solemnly. "Jeannie here didn't like them, but I was too dead-set to get to Daytona to pay her any mind." Shelly paused and looked at her friend, who stared at Lucy sadly. "They dumped us in a swamp," she finished quietly.

Lucy sat speechless while the various ghosts shifted nervously. Harry looked at her with a sorrowful expression.

"Not everyone is going to have a happy story," he said quietly. "Can you manage that?"

After a moment's hesitation, Lucy nodded and then picked up the script. A collective sigh of relief could be heard in the room as she read aloud. "My name is Lucy, and I'm calling with some information on the disappearance of state-the-name. It has come to my knowledge that state-the-name was state-the-nature-of-the-disappearance, and his/her remains cannot be recovered/can be recovered from this location. Give personal message. Answer questions."

Lucy looked up at Harry, who smiled encouragingly. Lucy read the script again as if she were calling Shelly's family. "My name is Lucy, and I'm calling with some information regarding the disappearance of Shelly Martini. It has come to my knowledge that Shelly was murdered by two men from South Carolina as she was hitchhiking to Daytona Beach. Her remains can be recovered from a swamp just off of I-95 one mile south of the Virginia/North Carolina border." Lucy looked up, her face a mask of horror. "I can't read this! How do you say something like that?" She turned to Shelly and asked, "How do I tell your mother you're decomposing in some swamp somewhere?"

Before Harry could answer, Shelly cut him off with a raised hand. "Listen to me," she snarled, "You are going to call my ma, and you are going to tell her what happened to me. We might seem just fine to you, but believe me, being dead is hell. There ain't nothin' to do here 'cept watch everyone we love suffer for our sake. And we can't do a damn thing about it. Now if you can't do it for me, do it for all the other girls those two shitheels will hurt when they git the chance." Shelly's voice broke. "You have to do this," she sobbed. "You *have* to." Jeannie stared at Lucy sorrowfully as Shelly turned into her embrace. She spoke quietly over the weeping girl's head.

"Please help us," she begged, her voice choked with emotion. "We *are* suffering; our families are suffering. You are the only one who can give us closure."

Any thoughts of backing out fled in the face of the young woman's grief. With new resolve, Lucy picked up the phone and dialed the number Shelly had given Harry. According to the list, Shelly and Jeannie had been missing for only a few months. At the back of her mind, Lucy knew that after such a short time, the families of the two girls were most likely deep into their grief, or worse, holding on to the hope that their daughters might still be alive. Lucy looked up to find Harry's expression echoing her thoughts. His face seemed to frown and smile at the same time, his eyes sad. Lucy turned back to the script, mentally rehearsing as the phone on the other end continued to ring. After the sixth ring, an answering machine picked up.

"You have reached the Martini-Able residence. We are currently not accepting any calls at this number. If you are calling with any information regarding Shelly, please contact the Stafford County Sheriff's Department at seven-zero-three five-five-five four-six-three-six." The recording ended abruptly without the beep to indicate that a message could be left. Lucy hung up when the phone began to hum, indicating the line was open.

Shelly had ceased crying during Lucy's call and stood looking around the room dispiritedly. "That was my stepdad," she said dully, her face shimmering as if the tears had frozen to her cheeks in a sheet of ice.

"Don't worry," Lucy assured her. "I'll just call the number they gave and tell the sheriff's department instead. That would be better anyway, right? They'll be able to do something about it."

Harry frowned down at the table as the ghosts around the room shifted uncomfortably. Shelly shook her head, and then she turned back to Jeannie and laid her head on her shoulder.

"What?" Lucy asked, confused by what seemed to be a good turn of events.

"Calling the cops ain't gonna do us a bit of good," Shelly moaned, her voice muffled by Jeannie's shoulder.

"The police are usually less than receptive to what they consider 'psychic' information," Harry explained.

"But you hear all the time about psychics helping the police solve crimes," Lucy protested.

"I'm afraid that's been a bit exaggerated. They are more likely to write you off as some kind of loon." Harry shuffled the rest of the list into a neat stack. Then, with nothing else to do, he sat back in the chair and studied the cracks in the Formica-topped table.

"That's it?" Lucy asked, incredulous. "You spend two days convincing me to help you but then you give up at the first roadblock?"

Looking around, she got no answer from the group. "Good grief," she muttered as she picked up the phone and dialed the number given on the recording. It was answered without ringing. A carefully modulated voice spoke.

"You have reached the Stafford County Sheriff's Department Info Line. If you are calling to report a crime, please press one. If you have information regarding criminal activity, please press two. If you are calling for general information, please press three. If this is an emergency, please hang up and dial nine-one-one. All calls will be recorded. To hear this message again, please press the pound sign."

Lucy pressed the two button and then waited through a series of clicks until the phone on the other end began to ring in an old-fashioned trilling. Harry and the other ghosts watched her, their expressions doubtful. Shelly peeked at Lucy from Jeannie's shoulder. Lucy stared around the room. She jumped when a deep bass boomed into her ear.

"Sheriff Perrault."

Suddenly uncomfortable, Lucy began to stammer. "I, uh, I have some information about Shelly Martini."

"Uh-huh."

Lucy was caught off-guard by the dispassionate response. "I know how she died and where she is," she blurted, and then she cringed at her lack of delicacy. The phone remained silent for a few moments before the sheriff spoke again.

"What's your name?"

"Lucy Godwin," she blurted before she realized that Harry and Shelly were both gesturing for her to hang up.

"OK, Miss Godwin. How did you come by this information?"

"Uh, I can't really say anything about that. But I do know that Shelly Martini and Jeannie Allen were abducted by two men about five months ago as they were hitchhiking to Daytona Beach."

"Yeah? You and everyone else watchin' *America's Most Wanted*," the sheriff retorted.

Lucy was shocked by his response. Suddenly angry, she snapped back, "Let me tell you what I know, OK? Shelly and Jeannie were murdered and left in a swamp just off of I-95 one mile south of the Virginia/North Carolina border. So you might want to find their bodies and inform their families that their daughters are dead." She finished in a near shout.

"Oh yeah, we'll get right on it," he sneered then the line disconnected with an audible, and insulting, click.

Furious, Lucy pressed the "off" button so hard the phone beeped in protest. Harry took the phone from her and placed it in the center of the table.

Shaking with anger, Lucy covered her face with her hands in an attempt to regain control of her emotions. George opened the icebox to fetch her another birch beer. Lucy dropped her hands to accept the floating bottle and pressed it against her cheek. She relaxed as the ice that had crusted on the bottle melted against her hot skin.

"It was as we expected," Harry said sadly. "We should move on to the next name."

"I'm sorry," Lucy said with a sigh. "Maybe we could try again later, find someone else to talk to."

Harry gave her a reassuring smile. "Of course."

Lucy put down the bottle with a bang and sat up. "Wait a minute," she said. "We can call Jeannie's family! Maybe they will be more receptive."

"I was a foster child," Jeannie whispered. "I was emancipated at seventeen so I could go to college early. If there is any family to tell, I wouldn't know who it would be."

Defeated, Lucy sat back and stared at the list. Harry moved it closer to her and then placed the phone next to it.

"We need to move on, Lucy," he said quietly. "We'll find another way to help Shelly and Jeannie."

Lucy sighed and picked up the list. "Who is Melvin Bissell?" she asked.

"Here," answered a very tan middle-aged ghost dressed in Bermuda shorts and deck shoes. "Lost at sea," he smiled sadly, gesturing at his bare chest that was covered by a pelt of graying fuzz. "Wasn't wearing my life vest."

Lucy smiled in spite of herself. She picked up the phone. After she dialed the number, it was answered right away by an elderly woman.

"Hello?" answered a tremulous voice.

"My mom," mouthed Melvin. Lucy nodded her understanding as she began to speak.

"Hello, my name is Lucy. I'm calling with some information regarding the disappearance of your son, Melvin Bissell. It has come to my knowledge that Melvin's sailboat was capsized twenty miles south of Caja de Muertos. I'm sorry to have to tell you this, but Melvin wasn't wearing his life jacket and, well, he didn't make it, ma'am."

Lucy sat helpless as the woman on the other end began to cry.

"I'm so sorry, Mrs. Bissell," she stammered. "I, um...I'm so sorry."

"Oh, honey, are you sure?" Melvin's mother asked through her tears. "Maybe it's some other Bissell you're looking for."

"No, ma'am," Lucy replied. "I'm sure. I have a message from Melvin. He says that he loves you and misses you very much and that you'll need to call Bob Russell to have the furnace serviced before the fall."

"Well, I'm not going to ask you how you know about that darn furnace, but it sounds like you've got the right Melvin," she laughed through her tears. "Is there any way I can have Melvin back? I mean, you know, his body," she asked in a discreet whisper.

Lucy looked up at Melvin, who shook his head. "No, ma'am," she answered. "The ocean has him now."

"Well, that's where he always wanted to be," Mrs. Bissell reflected sadly. "Thank you, dear. I haven't got much time left myself. It's good to know Melvin will be there waiting for me."

Melvin smiled, blowing the phone a kiss even as he began to fade. Lucy watched in awe as he seemed to fill with thousands of tiny lights. "He's going now," she whispered.

"Good-bye, Melvin," Mrs. Bissell cried over the phone. "Don't go picking fights with your daddy up in heaven now, you hear me?"

Melvin laughed, his face glowing. Lucy shivered as the small kitchen filled with Melvin's brilliance. All stared rapt as Melvin exploded into thousands of tiny lights that danced on the air like fireflies before winking out. Lucy found her voice as the last of the lights floated to the floor and then extinguished in an instant.

"He's gone, Mrs. Bissell."

"Oh, I know, dear, I could feel him go." Lucy could hear the smile in her voice. "Thank you again, so much. Good-bye, now."

Lucy stared at the place on the floor where the last light left a white spot on the gray linoleum. "Good-bye," she murmured.

Harry and the ghosts sat quietly until Lucy could compose herself. As if waking from a dream, Lucy shook her head, her body shaking off the goosebumps that covered her body. She looked around at the room full of ghosts as if seeing them for the first time, her eyes wide with surprise. Raising her hand to her cheek, she was surprised to feel heat radiating beneath the cool surface of her skin.

"That was amazing," she said, her voice shaking. Her guests smiled, murmuring their assent.

"We were hoping it would be a pleasant experience for you," Harry smiled. "Though it doesn't happen often, I think we've all seen someone pass over." Harry looked around the room to see many nodding. Lucy sat still in awe, unable to gather her thoughts. A few moments later, she found her voice again.

"I can see why you all want to go," she said, the quiver gone from her voice. "Well, let's see who's next."

# SEVEN

They spent the remainder of the day going down the list. Though none were as easy as Melvin's, none were as difficult as Shelly's, either. By dinner, Lucy was able to help almost half of the names on the first page, about eighteen in all. Most families were, if not happy to hear from Lucy, at least interested in the information she provided. A few reacted with anger, no doubt because of the nature of her call, but accepted her news as evidenced by the passing of their loved ones. By the time they watched the last of the lights trickle down to the floor, Lucy was exhausted and desperately in need of more aspirin to battle the fierce throb behind her eyes. Harry sensed her pain and quietly ushered out the large group of ghosts that still lingered. George stayed to boil some water for tea.

With her head pressed against the cool tabletop, Lucy willed the pain away. When she was able to, she looked up to see a glass of water and a small pharmacy bottle. Picking up the bottle, she read the label.

"Relpax," she read. She looked up at George. "This isn't mine."

George poured the tea, adding two heaping teaspoons of sugar. "Jeannie had the same kind of headaches you do. She thought that might help ease your pain better than the aspirin alone," he whispered so as not to aggravate Lucy's headache further.

"How'd she get it?" she asked as she shook out a small innocuous white pill.

"Probably lifted it from some pharmacy somewhere," George whispered again. "Little things we can get easily; it's the big stuff we can't do." George placed the tea in front of her. "Drink that and then sleep. You'll wake up feelin' fine." He gave her shoulder a gentle pat and then disappeared as Harry reentered the kitchen.

Lucy popped the pill and washed it down with the lethally sweet tea, gagging at the taste. When her stomach stopped roiling, she drank the rest down and then lay her head in her hands. Despite the caffeine, Lucy began to fall asleep at the table. Barely conscious, she felt herself being lifted and carried up to her room under the eaves. Harry laid her gently on the bed and removed her jeans. Too tired to protest, Lucy surrendered to his assistance. With great effort, she opened her eyes to see him pulling onto her a pair of flowered flannel pajama bottoms. Harry lifted her again to pull back the quilt and slid her between the cool sheets. He tucked the quilt around her, and after a moment's hesitation, laid his hand on her brow and disappeared. With her last bit of strength, Lucy lifted her hand to touch the spot where Harry's hand had fallen. Though it had felt like little more than a cool breeze against her forehead, her skin still tingled, and warmth slowly spread through her body. Lucy closed her eyes and fell asleep, a small smile curling the corners of her mouth.

It was dark outside when Lucy awoke suddenly to the sound of glass breaking. Wind whipped rain against the window panes, drenching the bottom of the sheer, white curtains where the window had been left open. Lucy sat up and listened. A moment later, another crashing sound came from the kitchen. Harry appeared before her, his face a mask of concern.

"It appears our young friend has taken offense to your new position."

Lucy groaned and reluctantly threw back the covers. With great trepidation, she made her way down the dark stairs to the kitchen. Halting in the doorway, she stood and stared in shock at the destruction to her kitchen. Most of the panes in the back door had broken when Jerry slammed it in anger. Glass littered the linoleum, deeply embedded where Jerry had stomped across it. Worse, Lucy's most prized possession, a genuine Meissen teapot, lay in a thousand pieces in the corner. Jerry sat and glared at Lucy as she stared at the crushed porcelain.

"Accident," he sneered.

Her face burning with anger, Lucy turned to Jerry, her fists clenched.

"Get...out...of...my...house." She spoke slowly so she would not be misunderstood, watching dispassionately as Jerry's face went white.

"What did you say to me?" he asked in a challenging tone, rising from the chair. Harry moved in front of Lucy as Jerry advanced.

"You heard me," she growled. "Get out of my house."

Jerry darted through Harry to grab her shoulders. At the same time, Lucy lifted her arms to shield her face, knocking Jerry's hand into her cheek. His fingernails scraped the skin around her eye as the heel of his hand connected to her cheekbone. Stunned, Lucy crumpled to the floor. At the sight of the bloody welts that rose on Lucy's face, Harry turned and threw a stunned Jerry across the kitchen and against the back door, shattering the rest of the window. Jerry landed in the glass that littered the floor, screaming in pain as the larger shards cut through his jeans. Harry advanced to inflict further damage on the other man but was halted by Lucy's voice.

"Stop," she whispered. Harry turned and kneeled next to her to examine the wound over her eye.

"Why'd you hit *me*?" Jerry began to whine. "I told you it was an accident. And you made me hit you, I mean...you hit my hand." Jerry glared as Lucy pushed herself off the floor. "It's your fault," he continued petulantly. "I don't know what you told Dave, but he's put me on the line permanently and cut my pay."

"Get out," Lucy said dully as she stood, swaying. Her cheek had begun to swell, and the scratches were dripping blood into her eye. Harry stood next to her, ready to catch her should she fall.

Jerry decided to change tactics. His voice took on a wheedling tone as he, too, pushed off himself up from the floor and stood to pick glass out of the back of his jeans. "I don't know why you're so mad at me. I'm not the one who almost got me fired." Jerry stopped at the sight of Lucy's bleeding face. He changed tactics yet again. "I'm sorry, baby, I just get so mad sometimes. Dave really has it in for me, and he's using you. He's trying to break us up. Can't you see that?" Jerry stood with his hands out in a placating gesture, crocodile tears pooling in his eyes. "I'll fix everything; I promise. Let's just go get some rest." Despite his best efforts, Jerry's voice took on an accusatory tone. "I've got to get up early, remember? I don't get to sleep in now like you do. Now, come on." Jerry approached Lucy and attempted to hug her.

Both she and Harry pushed him away, sending him into the table.

"Get out," she said more loudly. Lucy reached over and grabbed Jerry's keys. It took her a moment to twist off her house key as Jerry stood open-mouthed. When the key was finally free, Lucy threw them at his feet. "*Get out now!*" she shouted.

With as much dignity as he could muster, Jerry picked up his keys and went to the door, crushing glass and porcelain on the way. At the door, he turned and gave Lucy a baleful glance. "Feel free to call me when you've calmed down. Maybe we can salvage what's left of this relationship," he sniffed and then slammed the door behind him. Lucy resisted the urge to throw a chair at his retreating head. Instead she sat and allowed Harry to bathe the cut over her eye and hold the proffered bag of frozen peas against her cheek. While she sat, Harry fetched the broom and dustpan to clean up the glass. Tears began to flow, burning her cut eye, as he turned to sweep up the teapot. Seeing her distress, Harry stopped and sat next to her at the table. After a moment, Lucy found her voice.

"That was the only thing I had that was worth anything," she said through her tears. "My aunt always called it our safety net. It was worth a lot of money." Lucy fell silent as Harry reached out to hold her hand. After a moment, Lucy found her voice again. "My grandfather was in the army during World War II. He spent most of his time in France with a well-to-do family. By the time he left, he had married their youngest daughter, my grandmother. That teapot was their wedding gift. It was an antique even then." Together they stared at the ruin of exquisitely painted china. "My grandmother gave it to my mother. Since I was only five when she died, my aunt Frances put it away for safekeeping." Lucy paused as her voice broke. "I just put it out a couple of months ago." After a moment, Harry spoke.

"I'm so sorry, Lucy. If it weren't for me, none of this would have happened." Harry looked contrite.

"You had nothing to do with this," Lucy said vehemently. "Jerry's responsible for everything he does. He chose to screw everything up." Anger brought hot, burning tears to her eyes. Despite her best efforts, she began to cry again. Harry sat with her for a moment longer. Then he resumed cleaning. As he swept, George and several other ghosts appeared. Harry and the men conferred quietly for a moment. Then the other men disappeared leaving Harry and George behind to help Lucy. She picked up the broom and began sweeping. She had the worst of the mess cleaned up when they returned carrying a large sheet of particleboard from the cellar. Even though she could see them, it was still weird to see things floating through the air. Harry and George held the sheet in place, while another man nailed it to the door. When they were done, George took the broom from Lucy.

"Go take care of that eye, honey. I'll finish up," he said sadly. Lucy gave George a sad smile as Harry ushered her upstairs. In the bathroom, she stared at her reflection. Three scratches ran from her right eyebrow across her eyelid and ended at the bridge of her nose. Her cheekbone was swollen and already turning blue. Raising her hand, she touched it tentatively. She winced at the stab of pain that resulted. Harry pressed another bag of frozen peas in her hand and urged her to hold it against her cheek. Lucy sat on the commode with the makeshift ice pack to her face and watched Harry root around her bathroom for first-aid supplies.

"I can't help but feel like this is all my fault," he said as he sifted through a box of ancient medications and dried-out makeup. Lucy said nothing but silently hoped there was nothing embarrassing in the box like tampons or hemorrhoid cream. With a small cry of triumph, he held up a crumpled tube of antibiotic ointment and a mostly empty bottle of hydrogen peroxide. With the gentleness of a mother tending to her newborn baby, Harry bathed the scratches around her eye, wincing as Lucy cringed from the touch of the soaked cotton ball. After patting away the excess with a tissue, he liberally applied the ointment to her wounds. Then he sat back and surveyed the damage.

"Well, you'll have a real shiner soon. You might want to consider taking a holiday tomorrow." Harry said, his face twisted by a wry smile. As his eyes strayed over the purpling wound, his smile faltered. "I'm so sorry," he said again, his voice filled with emotion. "None of this would have happened had I looked for help from another."

In the midst of his apology, Lucy shook her head. "Then someone else's life would be a mess," she said. "Anyway, you did me a favor. I might have married him if you hadn't come along." Harry shook his head at the obvious joke and started to protest. "I don't want to hear any more about it," she interrupted, "and I don't want to talk anymore either." Lucy raised her and covered her cheekbone with the melting peas. "It hurts too much." She tried to smile but grimaced instead.

"I'll say good-night then," Harry replied, patting her hand. Then he disappeared.

Lucy exhaled an enormous sigh of pent-up anger, frustration, and sadness. She shivered as a trickle of freezing water from the melting peas ran down her arm and into her sleeve. Tossing the makeshift ice-pack into the sink, she went into the bedroom and sat on the bed. Her anger dissipated as sadness took over. Staring out the room's only window, her thoughts turned to Jerry. Though she had known for some time that it had to end, it certainly didn't make it any easier. Neither did it improve her chances with any other man in Paris. Jerry would see to that. He'd done it before when he and Mary Beth called it quits. Though she could never prove it, Mary Beth was certain he'd been spreading vicious rumors about her around town. She complained about it bitterly to Lucy until the day Lucy admitted that she had begun dating Jerry. Mary Beth had severed the conversation—and the friendship as well.

Lucy lay back on the quilt and continued to stare out the window at the stars that dotted the night sky. For the first time since her aunt had died, she felt truly alone. A small fist of fear clutched at her heart. Jerry was notorious for taking custody of his ex's friends after a breakup, not that Lucy had that many friends. She was not looking forward to the incipient loneliness. Her eyes heavy, she fell asleep before the tears could fall.

# EIGHT

Lucy awoke the next morning to find not Harry, but Shelly and Jeannie keeping watch over her. Shelly lay next to Lucy, reading an ancient fashion magazine while Jeannie sat at the end of the bed, fiddling with what looked like a jellybean.

"Morning," Shelly drawled as Lucy sat up, wincing at the pain in her head.

Jeannie looked up and smiled her greeting. She squeezed the glutinous bead until a golden oil oozed from a tiny hole at the tip.

"What's that for?" Lucy asked, as Shelly threw down the magazine to fetch a glass and two aspirins.

"It's vitamin E," Jeannie replied as she arose from the bed and carefully carried the weeping bean to Lucy's side. "It'll prevent scarring when the scabs fall off." With great care, she spread the oil across the scratches that had dried in the night. Lucy started at the strange combination of warm oil and the cold breeze that was Jeannie's touch. Shelly returned as Jeannie disposed of the now-empty pill and wiped the excess off Lucy's eye with a tissue.

"Here ya go." Shelly handed over a small drinking glass and two large blue pills as Jeannie went in search of a cold compress for Lucy's cheek.

"What are these?" Lucy asked, sipping the water while eyeing what had to be horse tranquilizers. Shelly picked up the magazine and sat cross-legged at the end of the bed.

"Percocet," Jeannie answered, her soft Southern accent floating from the bathroom, "It should take the edge off the pain."

"How do you know these things?" Lucy asked.

Shelly answered for her friend. "Jeannie was finishing up nursing school before...well, you know...before."

Lucy shrugged and, with great effort, swallowed the giant pills with the rest of the water.

"You should probably take just one for now," Jeannie called out before returning to Lucy's bedside. Lucy made a face as Shelly shrugged. "Oh dear," Jeannie said with a frown, realizing her mistake. "I probably should have told you beforehand. Well, you're going be feeling pretty loopy soon, so you might want to call your work and tell them you're not coming in." Lucy shook her head as she accepted the wet washcloth.

"I can't." Lucy winced as she pressed the icy cloth to her swollen cheek. "This is the first day I start working in the store. I can't call in sick; I really need this job."

Shelly shook her head. "Honey, you ain't lookin' so good. 'Sides, by the time them pills kick in, you won't be much good to them anyhow." Shelly went to the bathroom and returned, carrying Lucy's blue plastic hand mirror. "Here," she said, thrusting the mirror at Lucy. Looking at her reflection, Lucy's mouth dropped in horror. From her hairline to her chin, the entire right side of her face was swollen and tinged a deep purple. The three scratches had scabbed over, leaving ribbons of crusted blood cascading over her severely bloodshot eye.

"Yikes, I'll lose my job if I go in looking like this!" Lucy cried. She looked up at the two women. "But I'll lose my job if I don't go in."

Shelly and Jeannie looked at each other for a moment and then ushered Lucy into the bathroom. After a quick shower, Lucy submitted herself to Shelly's ministrations. Despite the occasional stabs of pain in her cheek, Lucy was impressed by the other woman's light touch as she skillfully covered the giant wound. Shelly sat back and eyed Lucy critically. With one last dab to Lucy's cheek, she handed over the mirror. Lucy stared at her reflection. With her meager supply of cosmetics, Shelly had not only covered the scratches and bruise, she had emphasized Lucy's eyes and lips with the makeup, effectively minimizing the swelling of her eye.

"Wow!" Lucy cried in delight. "You can hardly see it! Where did you learn to do that?"

Shelly smiled ruefully. "Don't let my bad dye job fool you. I might not be able to do hair, but I'm a whiz at makeup." Jeannie nodded solemnly and then held out two more pills. Lucy eyed them warily.

"What are these?" she asked before taking them from the other woman.

"Antibiotics," Jeannie answered. "I'm worried that the scratches might become infected. Your face is swelling far more than the trauma injury would call for. You're not allergic to any medication, are you?"

"Too late for that question," Lucy snorted, as she had already swallowed the pills. Jeannie smiled shyly and then moved over to brush her hair. Lucy closed her eyes as the brush moved rhythmically through her shoulder-length tresses. "Why are you being so nice to me?" she asked as Jeannie weaved her hair into an intricate French braid and then pulled tiny wisps around her face to further camouflage the damage to her cheek and eye.

This time, it was Shelly's turn to snort. "Mr. President told us to keep you happy," she laughed.

Jeannie shook her head. "That's not true, Shelly, and you know it," she scolded quietly. Shelly's smiled faltered and then shifted to reveal an expression of infinite sadness. Jeannie went to comfort her friend. She looked at Lucy. "Your calling the sheriff's department was brave. And when he treated you like dirt, you still wanted to help. Instead of freaking out on us, you seem to really care. A little makeover and hairdo are the least we can do in light of what you're doing for us."

"Don't forget the medicine," Lucy reminded her kindly. "Anyway, with Jerry gone now, it's nice to have someone to hang around with. Even if it's just for a little while." The three women smiled at each other companionably until Lucy noticed the time.

"Crap, I'm going to be late!" she cried, rushing to the closet to throw on twill pants and a white oxford shirt. With tennis shoes barely on her feet, she ran down the stairs to grab a cup of coffee from George in the kitchen. "You people are spoiling me!" She smiled as she blew the older man a kiss, and then she hurried out the door.

Lucy made it to work with only a few minutes to spare. Inside the bakery shop, Hannah was already stocking the shelves with fragrant bags of dinner rolls. She turned every time the door opened with a tinkle of the bell.

"Well, good morning sun—" she began as Lucy approached. Hannah choked on the rest of her greeting and stared at Lucy's face. "What on earth happened to you?" she cried.

"Oh, um, I did the silliest thing last night," Lucy stammered as she pulled a tendril of hair over her damaged eye. "I was too lazy to turn on my bedroom light and, um, I walked right into a...uh...door," she finished lamely.

Hannah's face grew dark as she stared at the younger woman. Lucy, in turn, watched as Hannah's scowling face moved in and out of focus. Without a word, Hannah turned and left the shop. Lucy put a hand up to her face and pinched her good cheek, which felt suspiciously numb.

Moments later, the rear door opened and Dave entered, followed by the still-scowling Hannah. Lucy stood quietly as Dave frowned at her. He turned and left without saying a word.

Tears welled in her eyes, stinging the cuts and making her makeup run. Hannah took her arm and led her to the front door.

"Go home, Lucy," Hannah said firmly. Lucy began to protest, but Hannah just shook her head. "Go home," she repeated. Then she closed the door behind her. Lucy made her way somewhat unsteadily to her car, only to find Shelly sitting on the hood, still reading her outdated *Vogue* with Harry and Jeannie nearby idly chatting. Shelly looked up as Lucy approached.

"Holy shit," she remarked as Lucy began to cry. Shelly floated off the hood as Harry and Jeannie led the now-stumbling Lucy to her door.

"What happened?" Harry asked as Lucy slid behind the wheel.

"I think I just got fired," Lucy sobbed quietly. The three ghosts looked at each other and then moved to surround their friend.

"I'm sure they're just concerned for you," Harry murmured as Shelly and Jeannie made comforting noises. Lucy pulled tissues and a compact out of her purse. Looking into it, she started at the sight of her reflection. All that remained of Shelly's masterful makeup job was a smear of mascara surrounded by clumps of waxy foundation that barely covered her now massively swollen face.

Lucy again put her hand to her face and closed her eyes. "I don't feel so good," she slurred. With great effort, she opened her one good eye to look for her keys. "I feel like I'm floating," she mumbled as she dropped her keys and then passed out. An alarmed Harry began to shake the now-unconscious woman.

"Lucy? Lucy, my God...Lucy, what's wrong?" he cried. Shelly and Jeannie just looked at each other and then back at Harry, their faces painted with guilt. "What's going on?" he demanded.

"We, uh, gave her something to make the pain more tolerable," Jeannie said quietly.

"What—what did you give her?" Harry cried.

"Just a couple of pills," Shelly answered. "It's just that she was only supposed to take one."

"Well, we can't leave her like this. What if someone comes out?" Harry looked around the parking lot and thankfully found it empty. "We're just going to have to drive her home. Jeannie, come sit on the other side of her and hold her hand to the wheel. You're also going to have to work the brakes." Harry nodded at Shelly. "You stay back there and hold her head up. Try to make it look like she's awake." Shelly shrugged. She lifted Lucy until she was sitting upright. Harry started the car and reversed out of the lot. After several stops and starts, the trio managed to drive the short distance through town to Lucy's house, even managing a floppy wave in response to the few greetings they got. With a collective sigh, they finally pulled into Lucy's driveway.

"Uh-oh," Shelly said as Harry turned off the car. "Nosy neighbor at eleven o'clock." The three ghosts stared at the middle-aged woman who was digging furiously in a weedy flowerbed. Mrs. Kelly had glanced up and waved as Lucy's car rolled to a stop. Now it seemed she was waiting to speak to Lucy.

"What are we gonna to do?" Shelly panicked. "She's gonna know something's wrong with Lucy as soon as we get out of the car."

Harry shook his head mutely as Jeannie looked thoughtful. "I have an idea," she said, dropping Lucy's hand in her lap. "I'll call her. When she goes to answer her phone, you two take Lucy into the house."

"Excellent," Harry replied and readied Lucy for a speedy escape. Jeannie disappeared into Mrs. Kelly's house. She reappeared moments later with the telephone number. She then went into Lucy's house. A second later, they could hear the phone ringing. With a glance toward Lucy's car, Mrs. Kelly dropped her gardening gloves and hurried to answer her phone.

As soon as the door closed behind her, Harry and Shelly managed to pull Lucy from the car and "walk" her to the back door. Jeannie had wisely unlocked and opened the door so that it was only a matter of opening the screen door and getting Lucy inside. Unfortunately, Mrs. Kelly chose that moment to return to the yard.

"Hi there, Lucy," she called out as Harry used Lucy's hand to open the screen door. Shelly turned and waved at Mrs. Kelly with Lucy's other hand. Then the two moved her into the house and slammed the door behind her.

"Thank God that's over," Shelly exhaled. Harry picked up the sleeping Lucy and carried her to her room. When he returned to the kitchen, Shelly and Jeannie sat at the table as if awaiting their sentence.

"Would someone like to tell me what all that was about?" Harry asked. Shelly and Jeannie said nothing. Harry glared at them for a moment before he spoke again. "No more 'prescriptions,' all right? Now I think it might be wise for you two to stay with her until she wakes up." With that, Shelly and Jeannie disappeared.

# NINE

Hours later, Lucy awoke, still feeling groggy and numb. With great effort, she swung her legs onto the cold floor and sat up.

"Next paycheck...," she slurred. She looked up to see Shelly and Jeannie helping her up. With their help, Lucy went into the bathroom to relieve her aching bladder and to wash the caking makeup off her face.

"Oh my God," she whispered as she looked up into the mirror. The swelling was almost gone, and her scratches were healing, but her entire eye had turned bright red with blood. Worse, it was now surrounded by a deep black and blue bruise.

"What's wrong with me?" she cried, staring at the gruesome image.

Jeannie gently examined her face and then sighed. "You've got a subconjunctival hemorrhage. It happens sometimes when people are struck or strangled...sometimes for no reason at all."

"Is it permanent?" Lucy panicked. "Am I going to go blind?"

"No, no. It won't affect your vision, and it should go away in a little while," Jeannie reassured her. Shelly tried to look hopeful but failed.

"Come on," Jeannie stated as she took charge. "Let's get you changed and get you something to eat. You must be hungry."

"Starving, actually," Lucy replied as she allowed herself to be propelled back into the bedroom. Though still feeling numb from the painkillers, Lucy was able to change out of her wrinkled pants and shirt and into a sweatshirt and twills so worn that they were almost white. After brushing her teeth, all the while staring at her bright red eye, she followed her floating friends down to the kitchen, where George and Harry and several other ghosts waited. Again, George had prepared a sumptuous-looking meal.

"What's this?" she asked as she sat down at the table. "It smells divine."

"It's a lobster omelet with Boursin cheese and anchovy capers," George beamed as he once again laid a napkin across Lucy's lap with a flourish. Harry sat next to her and tried not to look at her eye.

"Now, I know you didn't find any of that in *my* refrigerator," Lucy laughed, picking up her fork.

"I made a little trip to the market while you were sleeping." George tried to look innocent but failed miserably.

"What market?" Lucy asked, savoring the salty sweet blend of lobster and anchovies. "I'm pretty sure the IGA doesn't have lobster or anchovy capers, and I'll bet they've never even heard of Boursin cheese."

"I didn't say the market was here." George chuckled and turned to fetch Lucy some coffee.

"How're you feeling?" Harry asked.

Lucy put down her fork and eyed her friend narrowly. "How am I feeling? Hmm...how am I feeling? Well, for someone who's been haunted, beaten up, and then fired, all in less than a week, I'd have to say I've been better." With that, Lucy turned back to finish her meal.

Harry had the good graces to look guilty. The other ghosts stirred and then faded into the walls. George remained, however, to fill Lucy's coffee cup and ply her with homemade cinnamon rolls. As she finished the delectable meal, George also faded away, leaving Harry and Lucy alone.

Lucy could read the dismay on Harry's face and suddenly felt terrible.

"Listen," she said gently, "I don't blame you for any of this. Who knows? Either I've completely lost my mind and all of you are a hallucination, or it's all real and this is what would have happened anyway. Jerry's obviously a serious creep, and you are in no way responsible for that. So please stop looking like that."

Harry smiled and started to speak when the phone rang. Lucy jumped up to answer it and was surprised to hear Hannah on the other end.

"Hello, Lucy, honey? I hope I didn't wake you. I just wanted to make sure you're all right. How are you feeling, dear?" Hannah chirped.

"Hi, Hannah. I'm fine. I'm just so sorry I made Dave so mad." Lucy felt tears welling at the thought of disappointing such a nice man.

"Oh, honey, Dave isn't mad at you. It's not like you hit yourself, and he knows that. He is angry with Jerry, though, and that's why I'm calling. After you left yesterday, Dave had security escort Jerry out of the bakery, so I want you to keep your eye out for that young man. He's a nasty piece of work, and I wouldn't put it past him to blame you for his mess. Dave wants me to tell you to call the police if Jerry comes around. And as soon as you're feeling better, he wants you to come back to the store. He says he'd feel better if you're here where he can keep an eye on you."

Lucy was crying openly now, deeply thankful for having such wonderful people in her life.

"Don't cry, now," Hannah gently admonished. "Go get some rest, and I don't want to see you in here until you're ready. OK?"

"OK," Lucy said, sniffling. "Thanks, Hannah. Bye."

"Bye-bye, honey," Hannah replied. She hung up.

Lucy returned the phone to its cradle and sat down. "Well, it looks like I've got a mini-vacation," she said with a deep sigh. "At least I still have my job." Lucy looked down at the list of names on the table. Harry looked with her, and the two discussed which families she would contact that day. As if on cue, the room began to fill with ghosts again. George returned along with Shelly and Jeannie, and everyone waited expectantly as Lucy picked up the phone. Before she could dial, though, it rang in her hand. Startled, she answered it before the first ring finished.

"Hello?"

"Hello. May I please speak to a Miss Lucy Godwin?"

Lucy shrugged at Harry's inquisitive look and answered, "Speaking."

"Hi. My name is Matthew Brown. I'm an investigator with the North Carolina State Police. Sheriff Perrault turned your phone call over to our office since you had indicated that you had information regarding the disappearance of Shelly Martini and Jeannie Allen."

"Yes," Lucy hesitated, "Yes, I do."

"If you have the time, could you answer some questions?"

"Sure." Lucy shrugged at the gathering crowd of ghosts, and then she turned the speaker phone on so everyone could hear.

"Great. I appreciate that. Now, if you don't mind, could you tell me exactly what you told Sheriff Perrault?"

"Uh, sure. I told him that I had information about Shelly and Jeannie, that two men had abducted them about five months ago as they were hitchhiking to Daytona Beach. They were dumped in a swamp just off of I-95 about a mile south of the Virginia/North Carolina border." Lucy stared at Shelly and Jeannie, who stared back.

"Can I ask how you came by this information, Miss Godwin?"

"I really can't tell you that," Lucy stammered. "It wouldn't make any sense to you anyway." Shelly and Jeannie shook their heads in agreement.

"It would go a long way to verifying your story, ma'am. I'm sure you understand how important this is, especially to the families of the two girls."

"Family," Lucy corrected.

"Pardon me?" asked Detective Brown.

"Family," she repeated. "Jeannie doesn't have any family. The only people you have to contact are Shelly's mom and stepdad." Lucy started as Shelly and Jeannie began jumping up and down and waving their arms about. Even Harry was engaged in some weird sign language. Lucy wondered what had gotten into her friends.

"Now, how do you know that?" she heard Detective Brown ask. Lucy suddenly realized her faux pas and smacked herself on the forehead. Shelly sat and buried her face in her hands as Jeannie and Harry stared at Lucy.

Lucy covered the phone with her hands and whispered furiously, "What do I tell him?"

"I don't know," Harry replied. "I haven't the faintest idea what to do now."

"Miss Godwin?" she could hear him under her hand. "Miss Godwin, are you still there?"

Lucy thought for a moment and then answered. "I'll make a deal with you. If you'll just go and check out the location I just gave you, I'll explain everything. If I'm wrong, you can come to Ohio and arrest me. But if I'm right, then you'll know everything you need to. OK?" Lucy could almost hear Detective Brown considering her offer and waited for him to answer.

"Well, I guess I have no choice," he sighed. "I'm about twenty minutes from there. How about I call you back in an hour and we'll talk some more. That OK with you?"

"Sure," Lucy replied and hung up the phone. No one felt much like talking at that point, so George set about to make some lunch as the other ghosts milled around quietly. There was an unspoken agreement to halt all calls until Detective Brown phoned back. Harry sat close to Lucy as Shelly and Jeannie stared at the phone. Almost an hour had passed when it rang again. Lucy jumped to answer it.

"Yes, hello?"

"Miss Godwin?" Detective Brown's voice crackled over the line. "I'm at the site you mentioned. Are you able to describe it to me?"

"I've never been there, myself, but hold on." Lucy listened as Jeannie began to talk. "You should be on an access road that runs along the northbound side of I-95 before the last bridge out of North Carolina. The area is marshy, with trees growing out of the water and a lot of deadfall floating on top. You need to go about twenty feet into the marsh from the end of the access road. The water is about six feet deep." Lucy could hear Detective Brown giving directions to someone on his end of the line.

"Hold on for just a minute, please." Lucy put the speaker phone back on, and everyone listened as Detective Brown and whomever he was with slogged their way out into the marsh.

Moments later, Detective Brown returned to the line. "Miss Godwin? We've found something. Are you able to describe it?" Shelly and Jeannie looked at each other. Then Jeannie disappeared. Moments later, she returned, tugging on her shirt.

"A shirt? Well, it's more a halter top, really...white cotton with a sort of flower pattern, though it's probably not white anymore. Hold on." Lucy listened to Jeannie for a moment, and then she spoke again, her voice catching. "Jeannie is a little less than three feet to your right, underneath that large tree trunk. There's a cluster of water lilies and dead branches floating right in front of it. Shelly is underneath her. You might have to send a diver. Their bodies are tied to a garbage bag full of rocks." Lucy, Shelly, and Jeannie all began to cry. "Their backpacks are lying on the bottom of the marsh, right underneath your canoe." The squawk of a police radio echoed through the kitchen, and they could hear Detective Brown's voice calling for the diver and the forensic team.

"Miss Godwin, please stay on the line." Detective Brown had lost his friendly tone and now sounded curt and extremely official. Lucy didn't care. The enormity of the situation had finally hit her. It was one thing to know her new friends as ghosts, but it was quite another to realize that they were the victims of a horrible crime. Images of Jeannie's beautiful face dirty and bloated with swamp water came unbidden to Lucy's mind. She was fully crying when Detective Brown spoke again a few minutes later.

"Miss Godwin, please answer your door." Lucy hadn't even heard the doorbell. Taking the phone with her, she got up and went through the house to the front door. Through the window in the door, she could see a local sheriff's deputy just outside.

"Deputy Blont will stay with you until we are able to question you more fully." Lucy dropped the phone down by her side as Detective Brown severed the connection.

Lucy knew Mark Blont from high school, though they had lost touch over the years since graduation. He smiled at her as she opened the door.

"Hey, Lucy. You causing trouble again?" he asked as she stepped aside to let him in. He looked around with a practiced eye, and then he glanced back at Lucy. He did a double take when he spotted her eye and gave a low whistle. He mistakenly attributed her grief to her injury.

"Anything you want to tell me?" he asked as he looked from her face to the boarded-up back door. Lucy shook her head and closed the door behind him. She felt more than saw Harry appear beside her, and she was grateful that he was nearby, even if it was only in spirit. Together they watched as Mark carefully crossed the small living room to the kitchen, looking at everything but the ghosts that remained scattered throughout. Lucy followed him into the kitchen, where he sat down at the table, still looking at the boarded-up door.

"Your lock wasn't forced, but your windows are all broken. I'll assume you knew the person who assaulted you?" he asked as he pulled a small notebook and pen out of his pocket.

Lucy went to the refrigerator, pulled out two birch beers, and set them on the table. Then she sat down across from him as Harry took the other seat. Jeannie and Shelly stood to one side both of them, looking at Mark with varying degrees of concern. He continued to look at Lucy with his pen poised at the ready.

"I'm not going to file a report," she said as she shook her head. "It's over now."

Mark sighed and put his notebook and pen back into his pocket. "You know, Lucy, there's nothing to be gained by protecting him. Men who hit women don't deserve the loyalty they are given. And if you're worried about him bad-mouthing you around town like he did to Mary Beth, well...let's just say his word doesn't carry a lot of weight anymore."

"Thanks," Lucy replied, smiling sadly. "But I'm still not going to file a report." Mark started to say something, but Lucy put her hand up and interrupted him. "It's not because I'm protecting him...or that other thing. I just want it to go away. And...as far as I know...it has."

Harry shook his head, and Mark unknowingly followed suit. "Fine, but if it happens again, I want you to call me. Deal?" he said sternly.

"Deal," Lucy agreed.

Mark opened the birch beer and then smiled at her. "So, what's up with this North Carolina thing? You causing trouble there now, too?"

Lucy glanced over at Harry, who simply shrugged. Then she glanced over at Mark, who, though much more amiable, hadn't quite lost his cop look. "I guess they want to ask me some questions," she said lamely.

Mark twirled his bottle on the table as he regarded Lucy. "Detective Brown said it's regarding a double homicide," he said. He took a swig of birch beer. "Those are going to be some pretty serious questions."

Lucy regarded her untouched bottle. She knew Mark well, even though they ran in different groups at school. They had both attended the same church and had belonged to its youth group. For four years, they had gone both gone to the same Bible camps and mixers, and for a brief period of time, Lucy had had a crush on Mark's older brother, Tim. Where most teenaged boys would have teased her mercilessly, Mark had been sweetly understanding and had even gone as far as to put in a good word for her, to no avail. They were good friends then, and Lucy felt like she could trust him. She glanced over at Harry, who seemed to have read her mind. He gave her a small nod and turned to watch Mark.

Lucy played with the cap on her birch beer and wondered how to begin. Then she took a deep breath. "Do you remember Maeve O'Connell...when we were kids?"

Mark squinted up at the ceiling. "You mean the old lady who wandered away from the hospital? She died, didn't she?"

Lucy nodded. "Do you remember anything else about her?"

Mark looked at her for a long time. "Only that you were the one who knew where she was. Tim was one of the kids who was teasing you when you started talking to yourself. Or I guess I should say when you thought you were talking to her."

Lucy regarded him silently. He stared back at her blankly, and then it dawned on him.

"You think you see dead people," Mark stated flatly. "Like that movie."

Lucy winced. "Not quite, but something like that."

Mark leaned forward and clasped his hands in front of him on the table. Lucy watched as he wrestled with the idea.

"And this is why the cops in North Carolina want to talk to you?" he asked grimly.

Lucy nodded.

Mark chewed this over, and then he appeared to come to a decision.

"All right," he said as he slapped the table. "How about you start at the beginning."

Lucy and all the ghosts let out a collective sigh of relief. She smiled inwardly as Mark shivered at the sudden change in temperature, and then she began her story.

An hour later, Mark stared at her, his eyes wide, as she finished. Everyone watched him expectantly as he sat back.

All he could say was, "Wow."

Lucy just shrugged.

"So you're telling me that there are ghosts, all around me, right now?" he asked hesitantly.

Lucy looked around the room and counted. "Uh-huh. There's more than a dozen in here, right now, and there's probably that many in the living room, too."

"And Harry Truman's one of them?" Mark looked confused. Harry put his hand over his eyes and shook his head as Jeannie and Shelly chuckled.

"Well, yes, but not President Truman, though he's dead, too."

"And they can travel anywhere at any time?"

Lucy nodded. "Yes, why...do you want to test them?"

Mark rubbed his chin as he thought that one over. "Sure, that would go a long way toward confirming your story. Let's see...how about you send one of them to my house to tell me what I got in the mail today. It's at six-one-one-one Pine Avenue." Lucy looked at Harry, who looked over at George, who gave them a thumbs up and disappeared. Mark sat watching her. "Don't you have to tell them?" he asked.

Lucy looked at him oddly. "Why? They can hear you."

Moments later, George returned and described Mark's mail. "Your mail was in a pile on a table just inside your front door. You got a phone bill, an electric bill, a menu from Flying Pizza, one of those coupon packets, something from Clark County Extension Service, a letter from the FOP, and an application for a MasterCard," Lucy repeated.

Mark sat up quickly. He looked at Lucy more closely. "How did you know that? Were you in my house?"

Lucy smiled. "George is very good at finding out things." She gave George a sweet smile, which made him blush, sort of. Harry laughed. Suddenly George leaned over and twirled Mark's birch beer bottle, which sent it spinning across the table into Mark's lap.

Speechless, Mark stared at the bottle in his hands and shook his head. Lucy glanced at the clock, and then she got up to make something for them to eat. Behind her, she could hear him tapping the bottle in a rapid staccato on the tabletop. Then she heard him get up to check the back door. She and George looked at each other and laughed silently as they prepared soup and sandwiches. Mark returned to his seat as Lucy placed dinner on the table.

"Lucy...have you ever seen anyone, or talked to anyone about this... thing that you can do?" Mark asked.

Lucy shook her head. "No. Aunt Francis kind of ignored it after Mrs. O'Connell was found, and it's never really been an issue since nothing really happens here."

"Are you experiencing other things?" he asked carefully, "like depression or anger? Or are you having a hard time concentrating on things?"

"No," Lucy answered. "Nothing like that. I'm not crazy, you know. At least I don't think so."

"You know, that's why Tim didn't want to go out with you. He said anyone who talked to dead people must be crazy," Mark said as he stared at the clam chowder Lucy had set in front of him.

Lucy sat down across from him and made a face. "You know, I kind of resent that. People talk to their dogs, or cats...even their plants, and nobody calls them crazy."

Mark gave her a look. "Yeah, but they don't claim that their dogs or cats or plants talk back."

"What about all those people who say Jesus talks to them? They're praised for being faithful, but *I'm* crazy."

"Valid point," Harry laughed. Lucy smiled over at him and began to eat. Mark sat and stared at his food until the aroma got the best of him.

"So, is one of your ghosts a chef?" he asked through a mouth full of marinated roast beef with horseradish on sourdough bread.

"Sort of," Lucy laughed. "He's a deli owner from New Jersey."

Mark choked on his sandwich. "New Jersey...deli...you mean Georgio Miglione is one of your ghosts? The Mob boss who disappeared like...ten years ago?"

Lucy shrugged and then looked over at George, who nodded sadly. "Well, yes, I guess so...though it wasn't the Mob who killed him. It was the husband of some woman he was, um, flirting with."

George shook his head. "No glory in that," he said regretfully. Harry leaned over and patted George on the shoulder.

"At least you didn't fall off a cliff," he said consolingly.

Mark regarded his sandwich. He took another bite. "Well, I hate to tell you, Lucy, but if Georgio Miglione is one of your ghosts, you're gonna have more than just the North Carolina cops wanting to talk to you."

# TEN

By the time Lucy and Mark finished their food, it was getting late. Mark sent Lucy up to bed and took a watchful position on the couch. Upstairs, she dressed for bed in relative privacy. Shelly and Jeannie were reluctant to leave her alone with Mark in the house. Lucy reassured her that he was one of the good guys, but Shelly wasn't listening to any of it. Surprisingly, Jeannie agreed with her.

"They're all bad, Luce," Shelly insisted. "All men. Even the ones who seem like they're gonna take care of you...sometimes they're the worst."

"I've known Mark for a long time. He's here to protect us...I mean, me. You saw how he was about Jerry. Besides, he's a cop."

"Lucy, you can't trust him. You can't trust any of them. You *have* to be careful. Let Harry and George stay in here with us." Shelly began to panic.

"I just don't think that's necessary," Lucy protested.

"Lucy, *please*. Just let Harry and George come in, even for little while. *Please*." Shelly began to cry. Jeannie put her arm around her.

Lucy shook her head and began to speak, but Jeannie interrupted her.

"Lucy, you have to understand, one of the guys who did...this—" Jeannie indicated their transparent bodies—"was a cop."

Lucy's mouth fell open, and she stared at them, speechless. Then she looked at the door uncertainly, torn between wanting to run downstairs to tell Mark and wanting to bar the door and surround herself with as many ghosts as would help her. She didn't know what to do.

"Harry?" she called quietly. He appeared beside her, a look of grave concern on his face. Lucy looked up at him.

"You heard?" she asked, and he nodded.

"I think you should tell him," he said quietly. Jeannie and Shelly began to protest immediately, but he interrupted them and turned back to Lucy. "I think we can trust him." Lucy liked that he'd said "we." With more resolve than she felt, Lucy stood and walked out of the bedroom.

Downstairs she found Mark on the couch, blissfully unaware that Georgio Miglione, the Mob boss, was sitting right next to him. Mark stared pensively at the front door. He looked over as Lucy came down the stairs then paused at the threshold.

"What's up, Lucy?" Mark smiled.

"Have you ever known any bad cops?" she asked nervously. The smile left his face, and his expression went wary. Then he shrugged.

"A community of police officers is no different from a community of other people," he answered cautiously. "For the most part, they're good...decent, I mean. But just like any population of people, there are some bad ones...sometimes really bad. Why?"

Lucy could tell by the look on his face that his radar was up. She looked over at Shelly and Jeannie and then at Harry.

"Go ahead, Lucy," Harry urged. "Tell him."

Lucy sat down in the chair across from Mark and took comfort as Harry's hand fell on her shoulder.

"The detective in North Carolina is going to ask about the deaths of two girls. Jeannie Allen and Shelly Martini." Lucy then took a deep breath. "One of their murderers was a cop."

Mark looked at her long and hard. "Are you sure?"

Lucy shook her head. "I'm not sure...but they are."

Mark involuntarily glanced around as if Lucy's ghosts might suddenly appear to him. Then he leaned his head against the back of the couch and stared up at the ceiling. After a very long minute, he appeared to come to some sort of a decision. Mark got up and went to the door. "I'll be right back," he said, and he walked out into the dark.

Lucy thought he might be leaving, but he returned only moments later carrying a notebook and a tape recorder, which he set on the coffee table as he sat down. He said nothing as he scribbled something into the notebook. A few minutes later, there was a knock on the door. Lucy moved to answer it, but Mark put out his hand and got up instead. When he opened the door, Lucy was surprised to see another deputy standing there. Mark let him in, and he, too, looked around her tiny house as if taking stock of the situation.

"Lucy, this is Jeff Acco. He's going to witness our conversation," Mark said as he closed the door behind him. Lucy smiled uneasily at the serious young man. He declined Mark's offer to take a seat and chose to stand just inside the door.

Mark sat down and started the tape recorder. He made a few references to the date and time and names of the persons present.

"Now, Lucy," he began, "please describe the events of the last several days leading up to the present."

Lucy was so nervous that she began to tremble as she started to retell her strange and unbelievable story. To his credit, Deputy Acco remained expressionless and very professional, even as she admitted to seeing ghosts. For some reason, she found this comforting. She relaxed as she finished her version of the events of the last week. Mark's next question caught her off-guard.

"Lucy, are Shelly Martini and Jeannie Allen present right now?" he asked, his tone very official. It was disconcerting to Lucy to see happy-go-lucky, lighthearted Mark so detached.

"Yes," she answered hesitantly.

"Could you please describe them—their appearance, clothing, any distinguishing characteristics?"

Lucy looked over at Shelly and described everything she could see, right down to the tiny freckle that dotted the center of her right eyelid. Then she looked over at Jeannie and did the same.

"Could you please ask Jeannie Allen to describe the events that led to her death?" Mark then asked.

Lucy listened as Jeannie began speaking. After a few words, she began repeating Jeannie, like a spiritual interpreter. Lucy looked at Deputy Acco when they were done. His expression remained blank, but his eyes had grown wide.

"Can Shelly Martini corroborate Jeannie's account?" Mark asked as he made more notes in the notebook.

Lucy looked over at Shelly, who nodded.

"Yes," Lucy answered. Mark nodded silently as he continued to write.

"Could you please ask Jeannie Allen to describe the perpetrators?"

Once again, Jeannie began speaking with Lucy translating. Shelly then offered her corroboration before Mark could ask. He looked up and said, "Thank you" with the first smile she'd seen in several hours. Then his tape recorder clicked, indicating the tape was finished. His smile vanished as he reached over and replaced it.

"Now…" he began as he looked through his notes, "do Jeannie Allen or Shelly Martini know the current whereabouts of their murderers?"

Jeannie disappeared for a moment. Then she reappeared. "Rob Carmody is drinking in a bar called the Wagon Wheel in Commerce, Georgia, and Bryce Milton is asleep in a trailer at the Summit View Trailer Park in Waltsburg, North Carolina," Lucy answered.

Mark looked up. "And which one is the cop?" Jeannie answered.

"Bryce Milton," Lucy answered.

"Are Jeannie Allen or Shelly Martini aware of any evidence that might corroborate their story?" he asked.

Lucy looked over at Jeannie, who shook her head.

"They took pictures," Shelly blurted, "of Jeannie...after she was dead." A look of shock mixed with revulsion passed over Jeannie's face. Shelly looked back at her apologetically. "You died first. You didn't see them. I'm sorry." Then she looked at Lucy. "Tell him Bryce Milton has the pictures of Jeannie taped underneath the top drawer in his kitchen."

Mark's mouth fell open as Lucy did what Shelly bid. Deputy Acco's eyes were so big they seemed to take up his entire face.

"Are you sure...I mean, is she sure?" Mark asked. Shelly nodded.

"Yes," Lucy answered. Mark shook his head and made a few more notes. Then he turned off the tape recorder.

"Why don't you go and get some rest," he said kindly. "The North Carolina guys will probably be here in the morning to talk to you. They might want to talk to Jeannie and Shelly the same way I did tonight."

Lucy shook her head. "They might not be able to," she said sadly. Mark looked up at her questioningly. "If they tell Shelly's parents that they found her body, then Shelly and Jeannie will move on, or pass over, or whatever," she explained. "I won't be able to see them or talk to them anymore."

Mark rubbed his chin as he considered what to do with that particular piece of news. Then he and Deputy Acco put their heads together and quietly discussed the matter. Lucy watched as they went back and forth, alternately shaking their heads and then nodding. Finally, they seemed to come to a decision. When Mark turned back to her, his face was drawn with fatigue.

"Go on up, Luce," he said as he rubbed his hand over his face. "We'll call them." Deputy Acco nodded at her and went out the door. Mark leaned out to say something, and then he closed the door behind him. He pulled a cell phone out of his pocket and walked into the kitchen.

Lucy watched him go. Then she headed upstairs to take another pain pill and go to bed.

When she opened her eyes again, it was quiet in the house, and Harry lay next to her, his eyes closed. Lucy regarded him openly, sure he was asleep. Up close, she noticed things about him she'd missed before...like the fine bit of scruff that covered his chin. She wondered if his beard still grew despite his death or if he'd just neglected to shave before he died. Relaxed, he looked younger, the lines around his eyes visible only when he was animated. In repose, his skin smoothed, and the lines of his jaw and the shape of his cheekbones were fine, like a figure cast in marble. He was handsome in a way that almost seemed unreal.

Lucy was so deep in her thoughts that she startled when the corner of his mouth curled up in a slight smile.

"You're not even asleep, are you?" she asked. Harry chuckled. He turned to face her, his eyes crinkling with humor.

"I'm sorry," he said, not sounding sorry at all. "You were just so intent that I didn't want to interrupt your study."

Lucy couldn't help but smile back. "I was just noticing how different you look when you sleep. That's all."

Harry's eyebrows went up. "Different good or different bad?" he asked.

Lucy shrugged. "Just different."

Harry smiled. "Well, you look different, too, you know."

"Different good or different bad?" Lucy joked.

"Just different," he replied. He reached over and touched the tip of his finger to the spot between Lucy's eyes. "You're smoother here when you sleep."

At his touch, Lucy frowned, and Harry's expression changed to mirror hers.

"Is something wrong?" he asked as he pulled his hand away.

"I could feel that," she began, and then she reached out to touch the spot between Harry's eyes. Those eyes grew wide.

"Can you feel that?" she asked, and he nodded slowly. "I couldn't feel you before, but I can...sort of...now." Lucy laid her palm against Harry's cheek and marveled that she could almost feel skin and the slight prickle of his whiskers. "What do you think that means?" she asked.

Harry shook his head under her hand and pulled her hand away. Then he pressed his lips to her palm. Lucy's heart pounded. Then it sank again when he returned her hand to her own pillow.

"I don't know, but you should probably see if you can go back to sleep," he said with a small smile. Then he disappeared.

Lucy stared at the empty space where he had just been, hurt and embarrassed. It was a long time before she closed her eyes again.

# ELEVEN

---

The morning was mostly gone when Lucy was awakened by a rumbling of male voices reverberating throughout her house. Still caught in the web of sleep, she thought perhaps the ghosts were arguing again. Then she realized that one of the voices was Mark's. Lucy sat up and rubbed the sleep from her eyes and quickly looked around. She was relieved to find that Jeannie and Shelly sat huddling together at the end of her bed.

"What's happening?" she asked, yawning.

Shelly and Jeannie looked at her and shook their heads. "We don't want to go downstairs," Shelly whispered. Jeannie put her arms around Shelly.

"Where's Harry?" Lucy asked as she pushed the covers aside and went to her tiny closet in search of a robe. Instead she found her jeans and a flannel shirt, which she quickly donned.

"He's downstairs," Jeannie whispered.

Lucy nodded and then went into the bathroom to comb her hair and brush her teeth. When she returned to the bedroom, Harry was waiting at the door.

"That Detective Brown is here from North Carolina. He's having a difficult time understanding our particular situation." Harry glanced over at Shelly and Jeannie and then back at Lucy, his face distressed. "Your friend, Mark, is doing his best, but I'm afraid he's unconvinced."

Lucy stood, still wondering what to do, until a knock at the door decided for her. Harry stepped aside as she crossed the room and opened it. Deputy Acco stood outside looking crisp and alert, as if he'd had eight hours of sleep rather than the three Lucy knew to be the case.

"The detective from North Carolina is here," he said politely, in a surprisingly rich tenor. "He'd like you to come down." Lucy nodded and was about to move through the doorway when the deputy put his hand out to stop her.

"Are...they...with you?" he asked in a low voice. Lucy looked behind her to see Harry doing his best to usher Jeannie and Shelly to the door.

"Yes," she answered as she turned back, "but they're understandably reluctant to see any cops right now."

Deputy Acco looked around as he considered this for a minute. Then he leaned over and whispered, "Can they hear me?"

Lucy nodded as she looked into the room at her friends. Then she waved him in and closed the door behind them.

"I understand that you don't want to face what you fear most," he began in his operatic voice, "but it's important that you help Miss Godwin convince them of the truth of her situation. Right now, they believe that she has a personal relationship with your murderers and are not accepting Mark's story about ghosts." Deputy Acco looked around, uncertain where to direct his plea, and then correctly assumed the chair to be the place. "They may even arrest her," he continued, "and

I'm sure you don't want that to happen." Then he shrugged. "Besides, they can't kill you again," he finished reasonably.

Lucy was about to speak when someone knocked on the door, startling all of them. She opened the door to see Mark standing there.

"Everything all right in here?" he asked as he looked from Deputy Acco to Lucy and back.

It was Jeannie who answered him. "Fine. We're coming down." Shelly started to shake her head, but Jeannie pulled at her and forced her to the door. They passed through Deputy Acco, who shivered violently, looking around in a panic. Lucy and Harry smiled at each other, and Lucy took the young deputy's arm. The three followed Mark downstairs.

The tiny living room was filled with police and ghosts. Lucy laughed inwardly as George maintained a menacing vigil over the group. One of the men turned at their approach.

"Miss Godwin?" he asked politely. He was one of the most nondescript people she had ever seen. She smiled wanly as he introduced himself and the two other men with him.

Lucy studied Detective Brown and thought his name fit him well. *His first name should be Sandy*, she thought as she took a seat in the chair across from the sofa. His hair was a light brown that was echoed by both his tawny eyes and lightly tanned complexion. He looked exhausted, and his expression was closed and unreadable, which made Lucy nervous. She was grateful when Harry moved to sit on the arm of her chair and laid his cool breeze of a hand on her shoulder. Lucy looked up at him and was rewarded by the immense kindness she saw in his eyes. Harry gave her a reassuring smile, and in his ghostly way, squeezed her shoulder. She was further reassured as Mark moved to stand on the other side of her and Deputy Acco took up position right behind Harry.

None of this escaped the notice of Detective Brown as he sat on the sofa across from her. She could tell that because this was a less-than-ordinary homicide, he didn't know where to start.

"Well," he sighed. He picked up a pen and used the end to turn on his own tape recorder. "I have to admit you're not what I was expecting when Deputy Blont here said that you were a psychic."

Lucy shook her head. "I'm not a psychic," she said quietly. "I can't tell the future or read your mind. I can't make things move by themselves." At that, Mark shifted a little and cleared his throat. "I mean...I personally can't make things move...I can just ask them to."

Detective Brown raised one eyebrow and gave her a skeptical look until George leaned over and touched the tape recorder in front of Detective Brown. Everyone jumped as it shorted out, sending sparks flying across the table. A small coil of smoke emerged from the hole that remained.

Detective Brown looked at that hole for a long time. Then he turned off his now-shattered tape recorder and sat against the back of the sofa. "Deputy Blont said that if we notify Shelly Martini's family, then you will no longer be able to talk to her...or Jeannie Allen for that matter." Lucy nodded. He nodded as well as he digested that particular fact.

"Are they present?" he asked politely and not a little uncomfortably.

"Yes, both," Lucy answered.

Detective Brown scowled. He looked at Mark. "Do you have a tape recorder with you?"

Mark nodded as Deputy Acco offered to get it from his patrol car. When he opened the door to go out, Lucy noticed that her entire neighborhood was gathered on the sidewalk across the street. She sighed as she rubbed at the ache in the center of her forehead. She turned back to Detective Brown. He looked as if he wanted to say something but remained silent.

Deputy Acco returned a few moments later and set the tape recorder down on the coffee table next to the smoking one. As he turned, he caught Lucy's eye and gave her his own reassuring smile. Then he took up his previous position behind Harry.

Detective Brown turned on the tape recorder and began to recite, almost verbatim, the same information that Mark had stated the night before. She was not surprised when he began with the exact same questions. In fact, almost every word was identical, and the questioning was finished quickly.

Detective Brown shut off the tape recorder and sat back against the sofa. Lucy tried to read his expression, but his face remained impassive. In fact, all three of the North Carolina detectives were looking at her completely deadpan. She could tell that despite George's demonstration, they were having serious doubts about her story.

"I fear they may need some convincing," Harry murmured into her ear. Lucy shivered as his preternatural breath blew across the back of her neck, sending chills through her body. She looked away from him, embarrassed by her reaction to his presence. Harry didn't seem to notice, though, and moved over to where George was standing to quietly confer with him. Jeannie and Shelly remained huddled behind Deputy Acco, staring at all the cops with undeniable fear. Lucy tried to catch their eyes as all of the nonghosts in the room remained silent while they waited for Detective Brown to come to some sort of conclusion. After a few minutes, he did. His next words were surprising.

"Our track record with psychics hasn't been too good in the past," he said by way of apology. "We've had success with only one woman. Unfortunately, she's not getting any vibes about this particular case. All of our other 'psychic' tips have come from nutcases and attention seekers." He smiled at her apologetically and added, "Not that you are."

Lucy's expression was pained. "Of course not," she said.

Detective Brown sighed as he rubbed the circulation back into his tired face. He looked at his now-useless tape recorder. "I have to admit, your demonstration has gone a long way to verifying your story...but I'm still having reservations about the ghost thing. We have divers completing the recovery as we speak, so we're certain you've given us the location of Jeannie and Shelly's bodies, but I'm not sure if we can act on the tip you've given us about Rob Carmody and Bryce Milton. And we need to let Shelly Martini's family know as soon as the forensics report is available." He put out his hands apologetically.

"You want more proof," Lucy stated flatly, and Detective Brown nodded. Harry and George looked over at Lucy and nodded. "Then you decide," she offered. "If they are able to do what you ask of them, then you'll know I'm not guilty...or crazy."

Detective Brown considered this. He looked around the room. "What exactly can they do?"

Lucy thought about it for a minute. "Well, they can travel very easily...anywhere you'd want them to go." She looked over at George. "They can move things." Mark stifled a chuckle behind her. "They can sometimes retrieve smaller things...and obviously break things," she said, nodding at his tape recorder. "And if they pass through you, you can feel them."

At this, three of the ghosts who were milling about in the corners of the room moved forward to pass through the three men from

100

North Carolina. One of the ghosts, a young man named Michael, who had disappeared while backpacking in Yosemite, went so far as to sit down where Detective Brown was currently sitting. Detective Brown jerked violently and quickly moved away from the spot where Michael remained. Michael laughed, and he passed through the shivering detective again on his way back to the corner of the room.

"It's how they find out about you," Lucy said by way of explanation.

It was Deputy Acco's turn to stifle a chuckle as the other man rubbed at the goosebumps that had sprouted all over his arms. The other two deputies reacted just as violently and looked around nervously.

"All right, then," Detective Brown said in a shaky voice. "How about this...you send one of them to my house. There's a picture in an old white photo album on the bottom shelf in my office. It's of two men. If they can find it and tell you what it looks like and what it says on the back...I won't arrest you."

Shelly gave a grunt of disgust. "Good grief, we ain't dancing monkeys."

Lucy ignored her. "They need to know where you live," she said.

"They need to find that out on their own," Detective Brown said slyly.

No sooner had he finished speaking than George gave a growl and moved over to sit in the detective's place. Everyone watched as Detective Brown turned pale and started to shiver. Then George disappeared, only to reappear seconds later.

"Tell him it's two guys with long hair, one with glasses, sitting on an old brown couch, and somebody wrote 'Mark and Carl, 1964' on the back," George said. Lucy passed the information on.

Detective Brown looked up at her. "The one in the glasses was my dad. He died in Vietnam. All right, then; you're off the hook," he said, laughing nervously, all doubt gone. Everyone sighed with relief, Lucy most of all.

Detective Brown stood up, took out a cell phone, and walked into the kitchen. Lucy could hear him ordering a search warrant for Bryce Milton's trailer. She smiled over at Jeannie and Shelly, who visibly relaxed. Harry returned to Lucy's side, and Jeannie and Shelly followed. Deputy Acco unconsciously moved to give them room.

Lucy leaned over and murmured to Jeannie, "You need to find out where that other guy is." Jeannie nodded and then disappeared. She was gone for several minutes, and she came back in a panic.

"Tell them to call the Georgia cops right now. That Rob guy's got a girl in the back of his van. She's passed out, and I can't wake her up."

Lucy jumped up and went into the kitchen, with Jeannie right behind her. Mark and Deputy Acco shrugged at each other, and then they followed.

"Excuse me," she whispered urgently. "Jeannie has something she needs to tell you."

Detective Brown said something into his phone, and then he held it away and looked at her questioningly.

"Jeannie went to find the other guy, Rob Carmody. She says he's got a girl in his van who won't wake up," Lucy said quickly. Detective Brown looked at her for a second, and then he said something into his phone, apparently wrapping up the conversation. He hung up and turned back to Lucy.

"Does she know where they are?" he asked, and Jeannie began to talk.

"She says they are traveling northbound on Route 441 near some-place called Cornelia, Georgia. He's got a faded black Dodge van, an old one with diamond-shaped windows in the back."

Jeannie disappeared again and then returned to give Lucy the license-plate number, which she passed on to the detective. Detective Brown jotted down the number in his tiny notebook, and then he turned on his cell phone to call the Georgia State Police and his own office. In the background, Lucy could hear Shelly freaking out. Luckily, the Georgia police did not question Detective Brown's assertions that Rob Carmody was wanted for questioning.

Jeannie would disappear every so often to give them an update on what was happening. Jeannie reported that the Georgia cops were fol-lowing him as he fled toward North Carolina, where more cops were waiting for him as he crossed the border. She disappeared yet again and returned to report that the North Carolina police had arrested Carmody for speeding as he passed into the Nantahala National Forest just inside the North Carolina state line. A quick search of his van had turned up the alive but unconscious girl, whose wallet revealed she was a student at the University of Georgia in Athens. That made Mr. Carmody's flight into North Carolina a kidnapping and a federal offense.

Jeannie disappeared yet again. She returned to inform them that Rob Carmody had not cleaned the black carpet that lined the back of his van and that both her and Shelly's blood could be found in its backing. Lucy shuddered with revulsion as she imagined the poor unconscious girl lying in the blood of countless other women. Detective Brown lis-tened carefully, and then he ordered a forensics team to remove the carpet for testing. Lucy stood and watched as he made call after call coordinating the arrest of both men. She knew she should feel some satisfaction that men who had hurt her friends were going to pay for their crimes, but the thought of the pain they had suffered made her sick to her stomach. Harry seemed to understand and tried to comfort her as best he could.

Detective Brown glanced at her expression as he wrapped up his call. He placed the small phone back into his pocket and then indicated that she should sit in one of the chairs. She did. He sat across from her and clasped his hands together in front of him. He looked at her closely and then gave her a grim smile.

"It's purely speculation, but the girl Rob Carmody had with him appears to be under the influence of Rohypnol. Do you know what that is?"

Lucy nodded. "It's that date-rape drug," she answered, and it was Detective Brown's turn to nod.

"That's correct," he said quietly. "Though we may never know for sure, it's entirely possible that Shelly and Jeannie were given Rohypnol as well. Do you understand what that means?" he asked.

Lucy shook her head.

"It means they most likely didn't feel anything," Mark offered, and Detective Brown nodded grimly.

Suddenly Shelly appeared next to Jeannie. "That's not true," she said miserably. "We were paralyzed, yeah, but we knew what was happening." Then she began to sob. Jeannie put her arm around her and pulled her close.

"Tell, them, Lucy," Jeannie said quietly. "They need to know that we suffered...how much we suffered. The Rohypnol causes paralysis and amnesia, yes. But our bodies still felt the pain, especially Shelly. The drugs had less of an effect on her, so tell them...tell them that she suffered the worst of all." Jeannie turned her face away as Shelly buried hers into her shoulder.

In a voice almost completely devoid of emotion, Lucy told Mark and Deputy Brown what Jeannie had just said. Perhaps it was because she was so completely deadpan that her words had more impact than if she'd cried throughout its telling. Both police officers looked at her stunned, as if she'd dispelled the only bit of comfort they had in this whole terrible business. For Lucy, she could no longer bear the pain of the situation. Her head pounded, and she was so tired, she felt like she could close her eyes and sleep right there in her chair. In fact, she did close her eyes and give in to the grief that had been pressing at the edges of her consciousness. In a short period of time, she'd come to care deeply about Shelly and Jeannie. She let the tears fall slowly down her face, too tired to wipe them away.

Mark looked closely at her and then moved over to Detective Brown and murmured something in his ear. Detective Brown nodded and turned back to Lucy.

"I want to thank you for your help, Miss Godwin," he said kindly. "We're going to go now...back to North Carolina, but I'd like to talk to you again later, if that's OK."

Lucy opened her eyes and looked at him. "Won't you need me to interpret for Jeannie and Shelly when you get there?" she asked tiredly.

Detective Brown gave her a genuine smile. "No, that won't be necessary. You—I mean, all three of you—have given us everything we need to convict the two men who killed Jeannie and Shelly. Tell them we'll be calling Shelly's parents sometime today, so they'd best say their good-byes soon." He got up from the table and shook her hand. Then he and Mark went out to the living room to speak with the other detectives.

Deputy Acco stayed behind with Lucy, taking the chair that Detective Brown had recently vacated. Lucy looked at him and then closed her eyes again. She heard the front door open, and then close, and then she heard footsteps as Mark returned to the kitchen. With great effort, she opened her eyes to see him hunting through her cabinets for a glass, which he filled with water and set down in front of her.

"Detective Brown said we could go now that they've had a chance to talk to you. Are you going to be OK here alone?" he asked as he looked around the room.

"I'm not alone," Lucy answered as she took a sip of the water.

Mark smiled. "Right. Well, a deputy will be posted outside, and I want you to give me a call if you need anything, OK?"

Lucy nodded. Mark gave Deputy Acco a look. He jerked his head toward the door. The young man took the hint and got up from the table. On his way past Lucy, he stopped and laid his hand on her shoulder. Lucy looked up at him and gave him a small but grateful smile. Deputy Acco returned the smile. Then he left with Mark right behind him. Lucy closed her eyes, barely hearing heard the front door close behind them.

She was so tired that she barely registered the fact that someone had picked her up and was carrying her out of the kitchen and through the living room. If someone happened to look in at that moment, they would have seen Lucy floating through the air like a leaf caught on a breeze. She opened her eyes briefly and smiled as Harry looked down at her, his eyes filled with concern as he carried her up the stairs. In her bedroom, he laid her gently on the bed and pulled her quilt over her. Lucy murmured her thanks, closed her eyes, and gave in to her exhaustion.

# TWELVE

Several hours later, Lucy awoke to the sound of someone calling her name from very far away. She opened her eyes to see Harry lying next to her, his eyes closed, his nose only inches away from hers. She watched him for a moment, longing to reach over and kiss the end of his nose. The realization that she couldn't made her very, very sad.

Slowly, he opened his eyes and smiled back at her.

"I didn't know ghosts slept," she said quietly. Harry chuckled.

"I guess we do," he said. He moved over and pressed his cheek against Lucy's. She was surprised that she could feel the pressure of his face, and it wasn't cold the way his hand had been earlier. Rather it was cool, like the face of a living, warm-blooded man coming in from a winter day. But it was there, nonetheless. Lucy's lips parted to speak, but an insistent knocking on the door interrupted her.

Lucy got up and opened it to see George standing there, wringing his hands.

"They're going," he said urgently. "They must have talked to the parents 'cause they're going."

Lucy threw off the covers and followed George down the steps to the living room, where she found Jeannie and Shelly filling with light. Unable to move, the two girls beckoned to Lucy, who walked up to them and into their light. Jeannie and Shelly were crying as they hugged Lucy with glowing arms. Lucy, too, began to cry.

"Good-bye!" she cried. "I'm going to miss you."

Jeannie pulled away from Lucy and looked at her closely, even as her body filled with thousands of tiny stars. She began to speak, but Lucy couldn't hear her anymore. Lucy shook her head through her tears.

"I don't understand...I can't hear you," she said as she peered into Jeannie's eyes. Jeannie put up her glowing hand and brushed her fingers against Lucy's temple. Lucy shook her head, still unable to understand what Jeannie was trying to tell her. Jeannie placed her fingers against Lucy's head, even as she filled with light. Shelly interrupted her and took Jeannie's arm. Then the two of them surrounded Lucy and enveloped her with their light. Lucy inhaled sharply as her heart filled with an immeasurable joy. Every sense was filled with the two women who had become her friends. She could feel them, smell them...even taste them. Then as soon as it began, it was over, and Lucy was surrounded by thousands of tiny falling stars. Jeannie and Shelly were gone.

Lucy collapsed onto the floor and sobbed uncontrollably. Harry knelt beside her and put his arms around her. Together they sat, rocking back and forth until her grief was washed away with her tears. George ushered all of the other ghosts out and then left the two of them alone. Lucy looked up at Harry, who smiled down at her as he tenderly brushed her hair off her cheek.

"I'm going to miss them," she said sadly.

Harry nodded. "Me, too," he said. "Now back to bed. You need to rest."

Lucy let him pull her up off the floor and carry her up the stairs. This time when he tucked her in, he didn't stay. She smiled at him shyly as he squeezed her and then disappeared.

Lucy lay there staring out at the twilight, wishing she had the courage to ask Harry to stay with her. She cursed herself for being so foolish as to want a ghost to love her. She watched the stars begin to dot the sky outside her window and imagined that Jeannie and Shelly had joined them. New tears gathered at the corners of her eyes. She wondered what would become of her when they all were gone. She would miss George, certainly, and in time, as she got to know the others, it would be painful to let them go as well. But it was Harry who would be the hardest to say good-bye to. A good-bye between living lovers was really only a momentary farewell. There still remained the possibility of a reunion. But Lucy would have to say good-bye to Harry forever. Eventually, he would fill with thousands of lights that would scatter and then disappear. She knew that no measure of the joy that would fill her heart would make up for the misery she would feel after he was gone.

As she fell asleep, Lucy wondered if she was crazy...not because she saw ghosts, but because she thought...perhaps...she loved one.

# THIRTEEN

The following week, Lucy's mood deteriorated. Harry noticed and tried to make up for the loss of Jeannie and Shelly. He was especially nurturing, which only made her feel worse because now more than ever, the possibility of losing him made her more and more depressed. Even Hannah noticed the change in her when she phoned to say that Dave wanted her back in the store on the following Monday.

"Honey, you all right?" she asked. "You don't sound like yourself. You want me to come over?"

"I'm fine," Lucy demurred. "Just a little preoccupied." Lucy could hear Hannah's doubt all the way through the phone. "Really," she insisted. "I'm just looking forward to coming back to work."

"Well, I can ask Dave, though we weren't really expecting you back until next week," Hannah said cautiously. "By the way, how's that eye?"

Lucy leaned over and looked at her reflection in the toaster. "It's better. The red is all gone now...and the swelling, too."

"Well, that's just fine," Hannah said cheerfully. "Why don't you enjoy that free vacation you got there, and we'll see you next week. Rest up. Dave's got three field trips scheduled to come in for tours next week, so you're going to be busy." Hannah's voice was so cheerful, Lucy couldn't help but smile.

Lucy said good-bye. She hung up the phone just as George appeared.

"You hungry, honey?" he asked as he opened the refrigerator and pulled out ingredients for lunch. Lucy shook her head and sat down at the table. George gave her a sympathetic look. "You need to eat, sweetheart," he mourned in his rich baritone. "You're just skin and bones. How about a nice salad with smoked salmon and cream cheese sandwiches?"

"No, really George, I'm not hungry," she protested, but George had already begun preparations. She watched as he deftly chopped romaine and watercress for the salad as the cream cheese softened. "You should have been a chef," she commented as he shook oil and vinegar onto the fresh crisp leaves and then added salt and pepper.

George gave her a beatific smile. "I only cook for my ladies," he said as he set the salad in front of her.

Lucy stared at the salad sadly. "I'm going to miss you, George...not because of the food...it's just that...well, I'm just going to."

"You feel like you gotta say your good-byes now?" George joked. He gently stirred chopped salmon, green onions, and dill into the cream cheese.

Lucy glanced at her list of lost souls and then looked at George. "You're next to go," she said quietly. "If I don't say good-bye now, I might miss the chance later."

George spread the salmon and cream cheese onto a baguette and placed it in front of Lucy, next to her uneaten salad. Then he sat down and took her hand between his own.

"You feel like you need me around, Lucy. You just put me at the bottom of that list," he said kindly.

Lucy shook her head. "I can't do that. I won't be that selfish."

"Losing Jeannie and Shelly was a real blow for you, sweetheart. Go ahead, be selfish. Besides, the longer before I shake hands with the devil, the better 'cause I sure as hell ain't goin' ta meet Saint Peter." George laughed. "Now eat. I'm going to go see what I can scrounge up for dinner." He leaned over and gave Lucy a peck on the forehead. Then he disappeared.

Lucy looked at her lunch and began to eat. It was delicious, as usual, but she could finish only half of it. Harry appeared just as she was pushing the rest of it away.

Harry took George's recently vacated chair and looked at Lucy with concern. "Aren't you hungry?" he asked with one eye on her half-eaten lunch.

"I must have lost my appetite," she answered guiltily. "I'll finish the rest later." She picked up her list that she'd laid next to her plate and idly read through the names. When she read to the bottom of the list, she sat up and read through the names again. "Harry, your name's not on here." Lucy looked up to see him smiling at her shyly.

"I took my name off," he said quietly. "I thought I might stay awhile... if that's all right with you."

Lucy chided herself as her eyes began to fill with tears. "That's fine with me." She sniffed, suddenly unable to keep from smiling.

Harry looked around to see that the room began to fill with ghosts. Then he turned back toward Lucy and said, "You ready?"

Lucy nodded and picked up the phone.

# FOURTEEN

Lucy's vacation turned out to be a working one as she made her way down the list. Each day she got a little better at passing on information to the police and to families. She had even found an FBI website that listed missing persons, several of whom were on her list. True to his word, George would not allow Lucy to make the call to his family, opting to stay with her instead. But fate...and law enforcement...had other plans. On Friday, Mark stopped by on an official visit. Harry was away, trying to determine some means of getting Lucy her own computer. (George had offered to steal one for her, but she refused.) Still shell-shocked by the events of the previous week, Lucy let him in under mild protest.

"I wanted to ask you about your friend, George," he said as he sat at her kitchen table. Lucy looked at him blankly for a moment. Then it dawned on her that Mark's visit was an official one.

"You want me to turn him in," she stated flatly. George stood nearby watching Mark, his arms crossed across his chest, his eyes narrowed to slits.

Mark shook his head. "No, not exactly. I just wanted to ask him some questions." He fidgeted in his chair. "I've been reading up on his, uh...career, and since he's already dead, I thought, what's the harm in clearing up a few mysteries?" Mark put his hands out pleadingly.

"I ain't saying nothin'," George growled from the corner.

"He says he's not going to talk," Lucy paraphrased.

"Doesn't he want to see his murderer pay?" Mark asked.

Lucy looked over to see George shaking his head. "I ain't rattin' nobody out. 'Sides, he was a good guy, a regular guy, and I had it coming."

Lucy turned back to Mark, who looked at her hopefully. "Nope, sorry," she said with a shrug.

Mark looked crestfallen. "I didn't think so. His attorney wouldn't talk to me, either."

George dropped his arms and stepped forward. "Shit," he cried. "He talked to my lawyer? Ask him what he said."

"George wants to know what you said to his lawyer," Lucy said warily, afraid to hear Mark's answer.

Mark started fidgeting again. "Well, I explained to him why I was calling...that I knew someone who was in communication with his client and if he could tell me the circumstances of George's death." Mark put his hands out again. "That's all."

"That's all...that's *all*?" George cried. "Shit, Lucy, he ratted me out! Now they know I'm dead. I could go any time now. Shit." George began to pace around the room. Then he stopped and stuck his finger in Mark's face. "You tell him I ain't sayin' nothin'."

Lucy put her hand up to George. "Stop, George. It had to happen sometime. So it's sooner rather than later."

George knelt down beside Lucy and put his hand over hers. "I'm sorry, honey. I wanted to stay till the end to help you through this. Now shithead here has gone an' fucked it up." He shot Mark a dirty look and then turned back to face her. "But I swear, I'm gonna do whatever I can from the other side to help you, OK? I'll be there, Lucy. You won't have to worry. Between Harry an' me, you're gonna be all right." The mention of Harry made Lucy smile.

As if he'd been called, Harry appeared. "What's happening?" he asked, a pleasant but confused smile on his face.

George stood up. "What's happening is Barney Fife here's gone and told my lawyer I'm dead. Soon as my wife hears...I'm gone."

Harry frowned at Mark. "Oh dear. Well...in his defense, I have to say he was probably trying to spare Lucy the trouble of having to speak with the New York police."

George shook his head. "Naw, it'd be the feds who'd wanna talk to her. He wanted to find out for himself...to be knowin' things himself. Now he's gone and screwed everything up...dumbass."

Mark looked around innocently. "What's going on?" he asked.

Harry looked at him. Then he turned to Lucy and said, "Ask him when he talked to George's lawyer."

"What good is that gonna do?" George asked.

"If he spoke with him last week or a few days ago, then perhaps the lawyer won't say anything to your family. If he spoke with him today—well, there's just no telling what might happen," Harry said reasonably.

George shrugged and looked at Lucy. "OK, so ask him."

"George wants to know when you spoke with his lawyer," Lucy said to Mark.

"Yesterday afternoon," he answered. "Why?"

"Because until yesterday afternoon, George's lawyer didn't know he was dead. If the lawyer tells George's wife, he'll be gone," Lucy said sadly. "He wasn't ready to go."

Mark stared at her as he opened and closed his mouth. He picked up his hand and put it over his eyes. "Dammit, Lucy, I'm sorry. I forgot about that." Mark dropped his hand and looked around the room. "Mr. Miglione, I'm sorry. I wasn't thinking."

George rolled his eyes at the ceiling and shook his head. "Dumbass," he muttered.

"Go and see what's happening," Harry urged George. "Then we'll have a better idea of how long you have." George nodded and then gave Mark another dirty look as he disappeared.

"What did he say?" Mark asked.

Weary, Lucy looked at him and rubbed her eyes. She was getting tired of being in the middle of their conversations. Her head was beginning to ache again. More than anything, she wanted to go to bed. Instead, she got up to get a glass of water and some aspirin tablets. "George has gone to find out if his lawyer has acted on the information you gave him," she answered as she shook out four of the mostly ineffective pills. Harry looked at her with concern.

"Maybe I should go," Mark offered as he got up from his chair. "You look like you could use some rest." Then he laughed ruefully. "Anyway, I think I've done enough damage for one day."

Lucy walked him to the door. "Don't worry about it. Like I said to George, it had to happen sometime."

Mark waved. He went out the door but turned back. "Oh, by the way, that Detective Brown called to say he'd be coming up sometime soon to talk to you. You OK with that?"

Lucy shrugged then nodded. "I guess so. Did he say why?"

It was Mark's turn to shrug. "Nope, he didn't, but if you need me here, just call, OK?

"OK," Lucy answered. She waved good-bye. She shut the door, turning to find Harry next to her.

"George says the lawyer is uncertain what to do with the news. He's going to keep an eye on him," he said. He took Lucy's hand in one of his and then placed the other on her back to propel her up the stairs. "Come on. Time for you to get some rest. I have a feeling this business is taking more out of you than you're letting on."

Lucy let Harry guide her up the stairs and into her bedroom, where he pulled aside her quilt. Shy, she climbed in, looking away as he pulled the covers over her and then lay down next to her. She closed her eyes and sighed. He gently brushed the hair off her forehead and cheek. Even as tired as she was, Lucy didn't want to fall asleep. She was worried that if she slept, Harry would disappear. With great effort, she opened her eyes to see Harry looking down at her with the strangest expression on his face. If she had a mirror, she would have seen that same expression on her own face. She knew then that Harry felt the same feelings for her that she was feeling for him. It was that warm, certain knowledge that without ever having to say the words, someone she loved also loved her. Smiling, she closed her eyes and fell asleep.

# FIFTEEN

The next morning, Lucy awoke in a panic, crying out for George. Harry held her as best he could to comfort her until George appeared.

"What's with all the noise?" George asked. He laughed as he sat down next to her and held her hand.

"I thought you were gone," Lucy sobbed. "I was afraid I didn't get to say good-bye."

"Aw, honey," George said soothingly, "I could never leave you without saying good-bye. You're like a daughter to me. You're my little girl... now, don't cry." George patted the back of her head and hugged her. "I won't lie to you, honey, it won't be long now. So stop that crying and be happy for me. OK?" Then he leered at her. "Besides, you callin' out my name's gonna make poor Harry here think we got somethin' goin' on." Lucy laughed in spite of herself.

Harry laughed along with her and pulled her up off the bed. "Come on," he said. "Get dressed. We're taking the day off." That was enough to get Lucy out of bed and into the bathroom in a flash. When she emerged, Harry and George were gone. Lucy dressed quickly. She followed a heavenly aroma down the stairs and to the kitchen. Sure enough, George was setting a plate of pancakes with spiced walnuts and apples on the table as she walked into the kitchen. Harry stared at the plate as if desperate for a taste.

"Yum," she said as she sat down and picked up her fork. "What am I going to do when you're gone?"

George turned around and winked as he cleaned up. "That's part of your day off. I checked at my lawyer's. He's not meeting with my wife until this afternoon, so you and I are gonna have some cooking lessons."

Lucy laughed, her mouth full of pancake. "I don't think I can afford to eat like this all the time."

George wagged his finger at her as he opened her refrigerator. "See this? You got lots of prepackaged foods that cost a lot and don't make very much. You buy the ingredients instead, you can make much better food for less, and better for you, too. You just need to learn to be creative."

Lucy doubted that but said nothing in favor of eating. Harry smiled as he watched her.

"I wonder what you'll be...when you pass on," Harry said to George.

"Burning, most likely," George joked. "I never got my absolution. But hey, it was fun while it lasted, right?"

Lucy and Harry looked at each other and then laughed. Only George could joke about going to hell. George laughed along with them as he picked up Lucy's empty plate and took it over to the sink to wash. When he was done, he turned and clapped his hands together. "Ready to go shopping?"

"I guess," Lucy said with a shrug. "Let's go."

They spent the rest of the morning at the supermarket, where George taught Lucy how to shop for basic ingredients like pasta and meat and how to check for ripeness in her fruits and vegetables. When George wasn't looking Lucy threw in three bottles of generic extra-strength painkiller to keep her nagging headaches at bay. She smiled sweetly when George turned to show her an international foods section she'd never noticed before. Aware that people were looking at her strangely, Lucy said little as she studied the various foods George was discussing. Harry tagged along, clearly out of his element. By the time they reached the other end of the supermarket, Lucy's cart was full of food she never dreamed she'd buy, half of it she'd never even heard of. She looked forward to getting home and writing down everything George had taught her.

Halfway there, Harry offered to check on George's wife to see if she'd made it to the appointment with the lawyer so that George could spend the rest of his time with Lucy. Lucy wondered about that.

"Shouldn't you be with your wife right now?" she asked as she pulled into her driveway. "This might be the last chance you have to tell her good-bye...somehow."

George shook his head as he stepped through the door and followed her into the house. "Naw, no point in it. Cherise wasn't much of a wife, to tell the truth. She blamed me when we couldn't have children then, when I had a baby with another woman, she refused to give me a divorce. The only reason she's got me stickin' around now is she wants to know where my money is. She don't know I parked it offshore in a trust for the baby." George rubbed his hands together and chuckled. "It might be worth it to see her expression when Goldman tells her I'm dead."

Lucy laughed with him. Then went to get the rest of her groceries. When she returned to the kitchen, Harry was back, and the two men took Lucy's bags from her. George emptied the bags and set everything out on the counter. Lucy hunted for a notebook and pencil to take notes during the second part of her lesson. Though Lucy already knew how to cook basic dishes like meatloaf and lasagna, George wanted to help her develop techniques for enhancing those dishes and possibly creating her own. Harry would watch for a few minutes, but then he'd disappear to track the lawyer's progress with George's wife.

Lucy was busy scribbling in her notebook when Harry returned from his latest visit. "She seems to be in denial. She's quite colorfully asking for proof," he said to George.

Lucy looked up. "Uh-oh," she moaned, "You know what that means." As if in answer, her phone began to ring. With a glance at Harry and George, she answered it with a cautious "Hello."

"Hey, Lucy, it's Mark." Lucy mouthed "Mark" to Harry and George, who nodded. "I know I'm the last person you want to talk to right now, but I have an Ira Goldman on the phone. He's your friend George's attorney. He's asking if you can offer any proof that Georgio Miglione is dead."

Lucy looked at George, who was smiling evilly. "You heard?" she asked. George nodded.

"Ask him to ask Ira why he needs to know," he chuckled.

Lucy did as George told her and then waited as Mark passed it on.

"He says Mrs. Miglione is desperate for closure in her husband's disappearance. She wants to wrap up his affairs." Then he lowered his voice to a whisper. "I've explained to him that once Mrs. Miglione gets her proof, George will pass over."

"I'll bet she loved hearing that," George said with a laugh. "You tell him to wait a minute. I got proof for him, but he's gonna have to wait."

Lucy repeated what George had said. She pressed the phone against her shoulder and looked at George sadly.

George took her other hand and looked down at her, his face both smiling and sad. "You're a good girl, Lucy. What I said before...I meant it. Nothin' bad's gonna happen, even with me on the other side...or next door...or wherever. Between Harry an' me, you're never gonna be alone. OK?" Lucy smiled even as the tears began welling in her eyes. George patted her hand and then let go to stand a few feet away.

"OK, you tell that kid to tell Ira to tell Cherise that the secret ingredients to my cure-all chicken soup are Louisiana red sauce, lemon juice, and...tequila." George started to chuckle even as Lucy passed on the message to Mark.

Cherise must have gotten the message because as soon as Mark finished repeating what Lucy had said, George began to fill with light. Harry moved over and put his arm around Lucy, and together they bid farewell to their friend. George's silent laughter filled her heart, and Lucy closed her eyes to fully embrace the great joy he emanated.

When she opened her eyes again, George was gone. From far away, Lucy could hear Mark calling to her. Dazed, she looked down at the phone in her hand for a moment before lifting it to her ear.

"He's gone, Mark. Tell them he's gone," she said sadly. She could hear Mark on the other phone and could imagine the reaction that particular piece of news got.

"Thanks, Lucy," Mark said. "I'll let you go now. I've got to deal with Mrs. Miglione. She's a little angry. Bye."

Lucy hung up and set the phone aside. She turned to see Harry looking down at her, as George had. "Are you going to be all right?" he asked.

Lucy nodded. "I'm going to be fine. It's just going to take some time for me to get used to these permanent farewells."

"Is there anything I can do?" Harry asked, still concerned.

"Sure there is," Lucy said, laughing. "You can help me put away all these groceries."

# SIXTEEN

Over the next few days, Lucy was able to help only a few of the ghosts, even with the aid of the library's computer. Unfortunately, more and more were arriving with so much hope and faith in Lucy that she couldn't bear to turn them away. Harry did his best to pare down the list, but each day saw the addition of one or two more. It was all she could do to keep up. By Monday, she was desperate to take a break and go back to work.

Harry opted to head to the nearly deserted library to see if he could make heads or tails of the Internet himself, so Lucy was on her own for her first day back at work. She was nervous as she walked in through the employee entrance, which was thankfully deserted. Lucy picked up her time card and looked at it, unsure if she should punch in or not. She hadn't heard from Hannah since her phone call on the previous Wednesday, and for all she knew, Dave had changed his mind about letting her go. She was staring at the time clock, chewing on her lip, when Dave poked his head out of the bookkeeper's office next door.

"Well, hey there, stranger," Dave said, smiling. "You forget how to punch in?"

"Hey, Dave," Lucy said awkwardly. "I, uh, wasn't sure if I was here at the...um...right time." She smiled wanly and waited for Dave to tell her she'd been fired. Instead, he looked at his watch and then at the time clock.

"Well, you're a little early," he said. "But go ahead and punch in. Hannah's gonna run you through a little field-trip lesson before you open the shop. We got one comin' in tomorrow, so you best get yer walkin' shoes on." Dave reached out and patted her arm and then went back into the office.

Lucy exhaled, closed her eyes, and offered a prayer of thanks for being blessed with such a great boss. With relief, she punched in and went down the hall to the shop. As she entered through the rear door, Hannah turned from the register and beamed.

"There you are!" she cried. "Let me take a look at you." Hannah walked over and laid her hands on Lucy's shoulders. With a practiced eye, she looked over Lucy's cheekbone and eye, tut-tutting over the faint scratches that lingered. "Well, you look worlds better," she said. "You haven't had any more trouble with you-know-who, have you?"

Lucy shook her head. "No, none," she answered. "That's over with."

Hannah beamed at her again. "Good. Now, you and me are gonna go on a walkabout through the bakery. We've got a bunch of fourth-graders coming tomorrow, so you'll need to know the drill." Hannah took Lucy's purse and jacket and stowed them in the cabinet under the register, where she kept her own things. Then she turned and hooked her arm through Lucy's elbow. "Let's go."

By the time they made it back to the shop, Lucy had to admit that the field trip was going to be fun. Some of the things Hannah had shown her even she had never seen before. Most of the observation platforms were off-limits to employees, so it was the first time Lucy had seen the giant mixers from above. Even her old stomping grounds, the packaging line, looked interesting from her bird's-eye view. She was further surprised to see Mary Beth smiling up at her kindly, when she fully expected her to be angry for having been given the job in the bakery shop. Lucy smiled back at her and resolved to renew that sorely missed friendship.

Back in the shop, Hannah opened the register as Lucy stocked the shelves. They did a brisk business that day, and by closing, Lucy was grateful to have a chance to sit down, even if it was in her car. Hannah waved at her as she drove away, and once again, Lucy thanked the powers that be for the people in her life. When she arrived at home, she was further pleased to see her house empty of ghosts. Harry waited for her in the living room, his face pleasant but apprehensive.

"Hello, you," he said sweetly as she collapsed on the sofa. "You look like you had a good day."

Lucy thought about that and then nodded. "I did. I'm tired, but it's a good tired." Harry smiled then got up and went into the kitchen. When he returned, he was carrying a tray of tea and cookies.

"Perhaps this will help," he said as he set the tray down on the coffee table in front of her. It didn't escape her notice that he'd included one of the bottles of pain killers. Gratefully, she took out three of the extra-strength pills and took them with the tea. It was then that she noticed the lines of worry that crumpled his forehead. She began to wonder about the absence of the other ghosts.

"What's going on?" she asked cautiously. "Where is everybody?"

Harry sat down across from her and clasped his fingers in front of his lips. "Well, we have a new addition to our little community...and you might say she's ruffled a few feathers."

Lucy looked around warily. "*She* has?"

Harry nodded grimly. "Yes. I've asked her to come at a later time, but I have to admit, I won't be sorry if she decides not to return."

"Oh dear." Lucy sighed as she sat back, holding her teacup close. "She must be awful if you don't like her."

"Awful is a rather generous term." Harry tried to joke. "I've never encountered anyone quite like her, but I'll let you decide. She'll be returning later to meet you."

Lucy rolled her eyes. "Great."

Sure enough, as soon as Lucy finished eating her dinner, what was soon to be her least favorite person, dead or alive, appeared through the front door. Lucy and Harry watched as a smartly dressed young woman walked the length of the living room to the kitchen, looking all around her. She smirked as her eyes settled on Lucy.

"What, the rest of your house get blown away by a tornado or something?" she asked snidely. Lucy's eyes narrowed as she studied the young woman who openly studied her. Like Lucy, she seemed to be in her midtwenties, with shoulder-length brown hair and dark brown eyes. She was exquisitely dressed in a tailored black suit, and for some reason, she was carrying an old cell phone. Harry coughed politely.

"Lucy, meet Whitney Butler. Ms. Butler, this is Lucy Godwin."

"Hello," Lucy said politely. Whitney smiled at her nastily.

"So, this is the person you think can help me," Whitney smirked. "Great, just great."

Lucy started to speak, but Harry moved to interrupt her. "Why don't we take down your information, and we'll let you know if, and when, Lucy can help you?"

Whitney looked at Harry and then pulled out a chair and sat down. Harry picked up a pen and jotted Whitney's name at the bottom of the list. *She'll be moving up real quick,* Lucy thought.

"So, how did you...uh...pass on?" Harry asked politely, pen poised over the list.

Whitney flipped her hair coquettishly and gave him a serious look. "It's all very tragic, really. I was on my way to a meeting at William Morris when I got mugged. They knifed me when I wouldn't give up my Blackberry...assholes."

"How is it your family doesn't know you're dead, then?" Lucy asked curiously.

"Because the fucking muggers left my body in some shithole warehouse in Staten Island," she drawled as if it were the dumbest question she had ever heard.

"How did they get you all the way from Manhattan to Staten Island? I'm assuming William Morris is in Manhattan," Harry said.

Whitney gave him a sarcastic smile. "Yes, it is. I had an, um, *appointment* on Staten Island before my meeting."

"Why didn't you just give them your phone?" Lucy asked curiously.

Whitney looked shocked. "What...are you high?" she asked, "Do you know whose number I've got in this thing?" Lucy shrugged and shook her head, at which Whitney gave a theatrical sigh. "Zach Braff, that's who."

Lucy hid her smile behind her hand. "Zach Braff? You died for Zach Braff's phone number?" she asked.

For a brief moment, Whitney looked uncertain and not a little bit disappointed that neither Lucy nor Harry was impressed.

For his part, Harry had no idea who Zach Braff was but decided not to ask lest he add to the already adversarial atmosphere. "Yes, so...how long have you been dead? Do you know?" he asked instead.

Whitney's face went blank as she considered this. "Well, let's see. My meeting was on a Friday, March seventh, or was it the eighth? Oh, wait...let me check my schedule." She tapped at the buttons on her Blackberry, to no avail. "Shit, my backup battery must be dead. Dammit." Whitney sighed. "The seventh, I think."

Harry jotted this down. Then he looked up. "What year?"

"What year?" Whitney repeated. "What do you mean, what year? This year."

"2015?" Harry asked, his pen poised.

"What? No, 2005. What, are you high, too?" Whitney looked at him.

Lucy stifled a laugh. "Didn't you know? It's 2015. You've been dead for ten years." She felt no small measure of satisfaction as Whitney's mouth fell open. Harry prudently hid his chuckle behind his hand.

When the confusion cleared from Whitney's face, what was left was a look of pure contempt. "Are you fucking with me? You think I'm stupid?"

Lucy shrugged her answer. "Go look at a newspaper if you think I'm lying." She was surprised when Whitney did just that. Harry and Lucy watched as she pushed away from the table and stalked into the living room where Lucy had left the Sunday paper on the end of the sofa. She rolled her eyes as Whitney spilled the papers across the floor in search of the front page. "You know the date is on every page." Lucy called out, but Whitney ignored her.

Harry shook his head sadly as Whitney yelled, *"Shit!"* When she returned to the kitchen, she glared at Lucy and Harry as if it was somehow their fault.

"Well, that's just great. I've been wandering around for ten fucking years? How did this happen? Huh?" Whitney glared at Lucy, fully expecting her to take the blame. Lucy glared back.

"Your fault, not mine," she countered. Whitney moved to retort, but Harry quickly interrupted.

"Let's see if we can't make up for lost time," he said reasonably. "Would your family be in Manhattan as well?"

"No, West Palm Beach. Why?" she asked, one eye still on Lucy.

Harry tapped the pen on his chin. "I think it's safe to assume that your parents don't know that you are dead, despite the fact that they haven't heard from you for such a long time. For you to pass on, we'll need to notify them."

Whitney snorted. "So, call them."

"Gee, why didn't we think of that?" Lucy retorted as she picked up the phone. "What's their number?"

"Hold on," Whitney said. She sighed and stabbed at her phone again. "What the fuck's wrong with this thing?"

Suddenly weary, Lucy pinched the bridge of her nose. "I think it's safe to assume that small electronics don't work in the afterlife." She sighed. "Off the top of your head, can't you remember their phone number?"

Whitney gave her a patronizing smile. "I'm a publicist, which means I have the numbers of, like, a thousand people. You think I can remember all of them? That's why I have this thing, and if I had my personal cell phone, I'd be able to call them myself."

Lucy rubbed her eyes. "Maybe you should go find your cell phone. I'm sure they'd love to hear from you," she snapped as she threw her phone aside and pushed up from the table. "I'll let you figure this one out," she said to Harry apologetically. "I'm going to bed." On her way out of the kitchen, Lucy picked up the bottle of painkillers.

# SEVENTEEN

Lucy awoke early the next morning with a raging headache. Luckily it was still early, and she was able to enjoy a quiet cup of very strong tea, hoping that the caffeine would help take the edge off her headache. Harry appeared just as she was getting ready to leave for work.

"I've been to the library to see what I can find on Ms. Butler's parents." Harry sighed as he dropped the list onto the kitchen table. "So far I haven't had any luck locating them. I may have to go down to Florida to see if I can dig them up...no pun intended." He walked over to her, put his hands on her shoulders, and looked at her closely. "Are you feeling all right? You look tired."

Lucy was grateful for his concern, and she gave him a crooked smile. "I'll be fine. Any reason why your new best friend, Whitney, has moved to the top of the list?"

Harry had the good grace to look awkward. "Well, she's rather disruptive. I think it might be best if we take care of her now. Don't you?"

Lucy chuckled. "You'll get no arguments from me." Harry laughed with her. He impulsively pulled her close, gave her a peck on the cheek, and then pushed her out the door. She made no objections; she was certain she was blushing.

Lucy was in such a good mood that she hummed all the way to work. She was still humming when she walked into the shop, where Hannah was industriously scrubbing the countertops.

"Well, don't you look footloose and fancy-free." She smiled as Lucy stowed her bag next to Hannah's under the cash register. "What's his name?"

Lucy jumped. For a brief moment, she wondered if Hannah had somehow found out about Harry and the others. She cursed herself for ever having said anything to Mark about seeing ghosts. "Whose name?" she asked cautiously.

"Why, the lucky young man who put that smile on your face, that's who." Hannah looked at her expectantly.

Lucy laughed nervously. "Oh, uh...I don't have a young man, I mean, boyfriend. I was just thinking I've got really great friends...and feeling a bit thankful for that."

Hannah gave a benevolent smile and then walked over and put her arms around Lucy. "Sweetheart, we're the ones lucky to have you. You're just the nicest girl ever, and we all want nothing more than your happiness." Deeply touched by her kindness, Lucy hugged her back and made good on that thankful part. Hannah squeezed her tightly and then let her go. "You'd best get a move on, my dear. You've got that gaggle of fourth-graders due here in about ten minutes. You ready?"

Lucy nodded. "I think I'm pretty clear on the whole process, but where do I meet them? Are they coming here first?"

Hannah shook her head as she tied on her smock. "No, they'll come in through the employee entrance. The shop's their last stop. Then they'll leave out these doors after they've had a treat." Hannah shooed

Lucy out the door. "Now, hurry. We don't want them wandering around on their own." Lucy retraced her steps back the way she came where, sure enough, two women were timidly peeking around the door as they held back a group of nine-year-olds.

"Come on in. I'm your guide for the day," Lucy said pleasantly. One of the teachers gave her a grateful smile.

"Hi. I'm Ann Baker, and this is Julie Kelly," said the older woman. Julie, the younger woman, smiled and held out the only free hand between the two of them.

"Hi. I'm Lucy Godwin," Lucy said as she shook Julie's hand. Julie looked at her curiously, still holding her hand.

"You live next door to my mother," she said in a surprised voice. "Wow, you look nothing like I thought you would."

Lucy didn't know how to respond to that, so she simply shrugged.

"I'm sorry. That sounded terrible," she apologized. She leaned over and whispered, "It's just that my mom thinks your house is haunted." Then shook her head and shrugged as if to imply, *Isn't that ridiculous.*

"Oh dear, I can't imagine what makes her think that." Lucy laughed nervously. She was relieved when Julie laughed, too.

"Me either." Then she went out the door and held it as Ann led about thirty kids into the hallway and asked them to line up along the wall. When they were arranged and relatively quiet, Lucy began the introduction speech that Hannah had taught her. It was a little long, and she wasn't surprised to see the kids begin to fidget. She was glad when Dave appeared for his brief moment of introduction. He was obviously uncomfortable talking in front of a group, so his speech was short and rehearsed. Then he thanked the kids in advance as he made a hasty retreat back into the payroll office.

Lucy watched him go and turned back to the group. "Well, what do you say? Let's go."

As she followed the path she and Hannah had traveled the day before, she found herself growing more comfortable in her tour-guide role. She was surprised at how much she knew about the baking process and gave herself a mental pat on the back as she answered all their questions. She was glad though that each department had a representative who gave a brief talk and answered questions, because they were becoming increasingly specific. During these brief sessions, Lucy stood at the back of the group and listened with growing concern as one boy's questions were being ignored. She moved to stand next to him and help him to be better heard when she became aware that he was considerably taller than the other kids and looked more like a teenager than a fourth-grader. When she looked at him more closely, she realized that indeed he *was* a teenager and definitely was not there for the field trip. She was about to whisper to him when she realized that too many people were close by. He didn't seem to know that she could see and hear him and participated in the field trip as if he was any normal, living kid.

Distracted by the presence of the young man, Lucy finished the rest of the tour quickly and then led the group to the bakery shop, where Hannah was waiting with freshly baked cinnamon buns. She very kindly let them snack as she told them all about how the shop was run. Lucy chose that moment to approach the young man who lingered at the back of the group.

"Are you sure you're supposed to be here?" she asked quietly, and then jumped as the young man jumped.

"Shit...sorry—shoot! You scared me," he replied. He looked at her closely. "You can see me?"

Lucy checked to make sure no one was paying attention to her. She nodded slightly.

"Wow, that's cool," he replied cheerfully. "You must get teased a lot, though, talking to dead people and all."

Lucy glanced over at him. "So you know you're dead," she said in a low voice. The boy nodded energetically.

"Yeah, I mean, I must be, seeing as how I can do lots of stuff I couldn't do before. You know, like walk through walls and fly. Flying's awesome." Lucy had to smile as he listed all the amazing tricks that came with being incorporeal. "And did you know that I can go anywhere I want? I even went to the Super Bowl. That was cool."

"Why are you here?" she ventured as the noise level in the shop increased.

The boy stuffed his hands into the pockets of his baseball jacket and shrugged, and then jerked his head back to flip an errant lock of brown hair out of his eyes. "My sister works here. I thought I'd come and visit her. Maybe apologize for being such a shitty...sorry—I mean bad brother." Lucy didn't say anything but looked at him curiously. He looked back at her with long-lashed brown eyes that looked vaguely familiar.

"I used to take off a lot when my dad was drinking," he explained. "Mary Beth had our mom to take care of her. She wanted to go, but I couldn't take her since she was only ten. How am I supposed to take care of a ten-year-old? Huh?"

"Oh my God," Lucy whispered. "You're Scott?"

The boy nodded, and then turned to watch as Hannah handed out more cinnamon rolls, much to the dismay of the teachers. "Yeah, why? You know Mary Beth?"

It was Lucy's turn to nod. "We were friends in high school." Scott smiled at her and then laughed as a cinnamon roll sailed through him and hit the wall behind them. Lucy bent down and retrieved the roll. "Listen, stay here, all right? I need to talk to you some more, but it can't be here."

Scott laughed. "No shit...sorry—I mean, no kidding. You don't want to look like some kind of nutso, talking to yourself and all."

Lucy nodded. She left to throw out the cinnamon roll and help gather up the students. Dave arrived to deliver a quick good-bye speech and then bid another hasty retreat as Lucy and Hannah wrapped things up. It was quite a while before everyone was cleaned up and out the door to the waiting school bus. Hannah and Lucy received many thanks from the kids, who seemed to remember nothing more than the cinnamon rolls. Hannah waved as the school bus drove away.

"There's something about fourth-graders that makes me tired," she said as she pulled out a broom. Lucy traded it for a stool, which Hannah sat on gratefully. "I remember when mine were that age. All talky-talky-talky, and then all of a sudden, nothing—not a peep."

"They are energetic," Lucy said tactfully as she began to sweep. Scott chuckled and surreptitiously kicked errant bits of cinnamon roll over to where Lucy was sweeping. She gave him a smile and then made her way around the store. When she was done, she was surprised to see the rather largish pile of food. "It makes you wonder if they actually ate any of it," she joked, and Scott laughed again.

"We'll need to mop in here before anyone else comes in." Hannah sighed tiredly, sliding off the stool.

"Why don't you have a sit down in the lounge for a bit?" Lucy offered. "I'll mop."

Hannah looked at her guiltily and then nodded. "Thank you, dear. I'll just rest for a minute and then come back and help you."

"Take your time," Lucy called out as Hannah left through the back door. Lucy waited a few moments to be sure that Hannah wouldn't hear her and then called out for Harry.

Scott jumped when Harry appeared a few moments later. "Holy shit...sorry—I mean...shit. How many ghosts do you know?" Harry looked just as surprised to see Scott.

"Scott, this is my friend, Harry." Lucy said. "Harry, this is Scott, our new friend."

Though still surprised, Harry found his voice. "Hello, Scott. What brings you to our happy little family?"

"He's from here," Lucy answered for him. "His sister works here...you know, Mary Beth? The one I was friends with in high school?"

Harry nodded. "Oh yes, I remember you mentioning her."

"I thought you could take Scott back to the house and talk to him," Lucy said as she pulled the mop and rolling bucket from the storage closet. "I won't be off for another few hours, and I can't really fill you in right now. At least not here." Harry nodded again.

"I understand," he answered. He turned to Scott. "Come on, you. We'll go to Lucy's and get acquainted." Harry turned to the doors in case Scott hadn't quite gotten the hang of the whole ghost thing. Scott waved at Lucy and turned to follow Harry.

"Why don't you fly?" Lucy heard him ask as they walked to the door. "You can, you know. At least I can. Maybe I could show you." Lucy smiled at Harry's deliberately patient look. "Did you know you have an English accent? Like James Bond. Do you know who James Bond is? He's like this spy guy, and he's English, too...."

She chuckled as Harry took Scott's arm and disappeared. Relieved to finally be alone, she set to the task of cleaning the floors.

# EIGHTEEN

The rest of the day proved to be slow, so Lucy offered to stay until the end of the day so that Hannah could go home early. Hannah took her up on her offer when Lucy promised to call Dave in if they had a sudden rush for day-old hamburger buns.

Such was not the case, and even Dave had to admit there wasn't much point in remaining open. Because Hannah hadn't taught her to close up the cash register, Dave came in to do it while Lucy checked the dates on the various baked goods and did some minor restocking.

"Take those to the back door for me, will you?" Dave asked as Lucy loaded up a small cart with the packages of bread, rolls, and pastries that would expire soon. Dave made a point of offering his employees the right of first refusal before taking what was left over to the local homeless shelter. Few people took him up on it, though, in an unspoken agreement to not deprive the people at the shelter of food. Dave gave them free product anyway and in sufficient quantities that none of his employees would ever go hungry. Lucy herself had a deep freezer full of enough bread to last her a lifetime.

When she returned, Dave had finished with the cash drawer and was locking up the store. "You go on home, Lucy," he said as he checked his watch. "It's almost five. I'll clock you out."

Lucy shook her head. He'd done enough for her. "No, no. I'll go ahead and punch out now and make up the half hour tomorrow."

Dave shrugged as he picked up the cash drawer and balanced in under his arm. "Suit yourself," he said. "Lightning storm tonight. Go home and be safe."

"I will. Bye!" Lucy called out as he went out the door.

She reached under the cash register to trade her smock for her purse. Then she followed Dave out of the store, locking the door behind her. By the time she made it to the time clock just outside the payroll office, the hall was empty. Lucy reached out to pick up her time card—and then realized it wasn't there. For a minute, she thought it might have fallen among the other time cards or onto the floor, but a brief search turned up nothing. She was about to panic when it occurred to her that Dave must have taken her card. Lucy smiled and shook her head. She considered knocking on the payroll office door but knew that Dave would either not answer it or deny everything. With another shake of her head, Lucy placed her hand on the door. She whispered, "Thanks," and then went out to her car.

As before, Lucy hummed on her way home until she pulled into her driveway. With Julie Kelly's words in the back of her mind, Lucy was keenly aware that her every move was most likely under observation. Though nothing appeared out of the ordinary, she tried to maintain the appearance of nonchalance as she made her way into the house. She was surprised to find it fairly quiet inside as well, with only Harry and Scott sitting at the kitchen table. Harry looked up and smiled as she dropped her purse on the counter. He crossed to the refrigerator for something to drink.

"We waited for you," he said when she joined them at the table. Lucy raised her eyebrows in question as she took a sip of her iced tea. Harry correctly interpreted her question. "I thought we could hear young Scott's story together...so we waited," he said by way of an answer.

"Some of it I already know," Lucy said as Scott nodded. "But it wouldn't hurt to hear it from the beginning."

Scott looked from Lucy to Harry and realized they were waiting for him. "Oh, sorry," he said quickly. "I didn't know you were ready." Lucy said nothing. Harry smiled at him encouragingly.

"Well," Scott began slowly, "I guess it all started when my dad lost his job at the truck plant, and we had to move into my uncle's trailer. Mary Beth was only like seven or eight, and I was eleven." Scott paused and chewed on the side of his thumb. "Dad hardly ever drank before then, but after that...well, he drank almost all the time after that. Mom went to work at that plastic factory at night when we were sleeping, but then they closed, too." Scott sighed. He began to pick at the hangnail he had started. "So anyway, when my dad drank, he either passed out or got really mean...like hitting mean. He never hit Mary Beth, though, because there's this thing in my family that you never hit girls. But it was OK to hit me."

Lucy felt awful as she watched Scott's face crumple for a moment. She and Harry glanced at each other but said nothing.

"So when he got like that...I'd just leave." Scott continued when he got his emotions under control. "Uncle Jack left a rifle in the trailer, so I'd take that and go shoot at stuff...like birds and squirrels. Mary Beth wanted to come, too, but I wouldn't let her. I told her she was too young, but really I didn't want to hit her by accident because I wasn't a very good shot." Scott stopped and stared at the table for a long time.

"What happened when you died?" Harry asked quietly. Scott looked up at him, embarrassed.

"That last time, Dad beat me up pretty bad, so I took my stuff and left. I was gonna hitch it to my Grandma Guthrie's house down near Springfield, but some guy on the road was being all weird. So I hid in the woods until he was gone. By that time, it was too dark to be hitching, so...well...there's this little cave I found nearby in the woods. I thought I could stay there and maybe they'd get worried and my mom would make my dad stop drinking and everything would be cool by the time I got back." Scott looked away and went back to chewing his thumb. "But I screwed up. I left the safety off the rifle, and it went off in the cave. When I woke up, the hole in the cave was gone. You know...the opening? And I couldn't get out." Scott caught Lucy's look of horror. "It wasn't that bad, really," he said quickly. "Like falling asleep or something. Then, when I could get out, I was like this." He waved at his transparent body. Then he dropped his hand and shrugged. "That's it, I guess."

Harry gazed at Scott, his expression a mix of respect and pity as Lucy closed her eyes and rubbed the spot just over her right eyebrow. Then she shook her head and looked at Scott.

"I never knew," she said quietly. "Mary Beth never said anything about what happened when you disappeared or what your family life was like."

"She wouldn't, though, you know?" Scott explained. "You were, like, her best friend and she really liked it when she could sleep over here because you had a really nice house. She'd never tell you anything that might make you not like her anymore."

Lucy was struck speechless. It had never occurred to her that *anyone* would admire her or envy what little she had. Mary Beth had always been more popular and certainly prettier than Lucy. That's why she'd been so surprised when Jerry asked her out.

"She was really crushed when you started dating that Jerry guy, too," Scott said, as if in answer to her thoughts. "I was there when she came home that day she found out you were going out with him. She called him a rat bastard and cried a whole bunch because she knew he wouldn't let you guys be friends anymore. She hates him for that."

Lucy shook her head. "I always thought she hated me for that," she said. She sighed. "Now I have to tell her you're dead. She's really going to hate me after that."

Scott shrugged as Harry looked on sympathetically.

Lucy sighed. She rubbed the spot over her eye. "Well, there's not much I can do tonight. I think I should go get some rest right now. I'll try to think of a way to approach Mary Beth tomorrow."

Scott smiled sweetly at her. "G'night," he called out, and then he disappeared.

Lucy turned to Harry, who was gazing at her pensively. "What's wrong?" she asked.

Harry leaned across the table and regarded her more intently. "This situation with Scott is much different than the others. Do you think you can handle that?"

"I don't see what you mean," Lucy responded with a slight shake of her head. "How is it any different than anyone else?"

Harry took her hand between his. His touch was no longer the cool breeze it had been before. Now it had substance to it, even warmth. Lucy stared as Harry entwined his fingers through hers and was momentarily distracted by the sensation. Harry didn't seem to notice the change. Instead he was studying her, his expression a mixture of fear and concern. It was another moment before Lucy realized he was already speaking to her.

"This *is* different, Lucy. You have to see that. You hardly knew the others, with the exception of Jeannie and Shelly...and George. This time it's personal...someone you know."

"Well, sure...if you put it that way, then it *will* be different this time. But what choice do I have? I can't not help Scott, or Mary Beth, for that matter," Lucy replied.

Harry appeared to consider this as he stared at her hand, his thumbs rubbing the very sensitive web of skin at the base of her fingers. Lucy shivered involuntarily and then looked away, her face hot with embarrassment. Harry still had not noticed; his face was a mask of concern when he looked up.

"Why not call Mark instead?" he suggested. "Tell him about Scott and let them look for his remains. That way you're out of it."

Lucy chewed on her lip as she considered this. She nodded. "All right, let's do that. I'll call Mark."

Harry let out a sigh of relief and sat back in his chair, letting go of her hand. It instantly felt bare to her, and somehow incomplete, as if Harry had taken part of it with him. Lucy covered it with her other hand, which was little consolation.

"Well, time for me to hit the hay. I guess I'll see you in the morning," Lucy mumbled.

Harry smiled at her so sweetly that all over again, she wished he still held her hand. "Sleep well," he said.

Lucy smiled back crookedly and then went upstairs to sit on her bed and stare out the window at the approaching storm. As she watched, a bolt of lightning turned the night sky back to daylight for a brief moment. Lucy began to count absentmindedly before she heard the distant roll of thunder, but her mind was not on the storm. Even when the rain began to pelt her tiny window, she was still lost to her thoughts. She began to count as the sky went black after another lightning flash. She rubbed the spot between her fingers, vainly trying to recapture the sense of intimacy she felt when Harry was touching her. It was no use, and Lucy gave up. With a sigh, she lay down on the pillow and watched the storm move across the sky.

She must have dozed off for only a moment when a particularly loud crack of thunder startled her awake. She looked out the window and saw that the storm was directly overhead, and rain was lashing at her window in sheets. She shivered even though it wasn't cold and moved to grab her quilt when she felt it moving over her. Lucy looked over to see Harry pulling it up over her shoulder.

"Just wanted to make sure you were all right," he said quietly. "The storm has turned quite nasty."

Lucy smiled. "I'm all right," she whispered.

Harry smiled back. "Do you mind if I stay?" he asked. Lucy felt her heart swell. She shook her head and then turned her face into the pillow to hide her smile. She could sense rather than feel Harry settle in beside her, and together they watched the storm.

Lucy was still awake when the storm moved off and the night fell dark and starless. She turned to see Harry staring at her in the dim light of the room. His expression was kind but serious.

"You're not sleeping," he said quietly. Lucy shook her head but said nothing.

"You should sleep," Harry whispered. "You need your rest. Just close your eyes."

Lucy gave him a small smile and obeyed. A moment later, she could feel a presence close to her. She felt the soft press of his lips against hers. She could smell the sweetness of sun-kissed skin and aftershave, as if in a memory. The pressure of his lips against hers grew urgent...but then left as suddenly as it began. Lucy opened her eyes to find Harry staring at her.

"I'm sorry," he whispered. "I don't know what came over me."

Lucy said nothing. She smiled. Then she moved closer to taste his lips again. As Harry moved over her body, she was so consumed with the feel of his body against hers, she didn't stop to wonder how it was even possible. She didn't even notice when lightning cracked the sky again.

# NINETEEN

Late the next morning, the storm was gone, and the sun was beaming in through the window as Harry shook Lucy awake.

"Huh?" she mumbled. "What time is it?"

"I'm so sorry, Lucy," said Harry, a note of urgency in his voice. "I let you sleep too long. It's after eight o'clock."

"Oh no!" Lucy cried as she jumped out of bed and ran into the bathroom. "I'm going to be late!" As quickly as she could, Lucy showered and dressed. Harry had a cup of coffee and a slice of toast waiting for her in the kitchen. He handed Lucy her purse and an umbrella as she flew out the door.

Even after surpassing all speed limits and merely pausing at every stop, Lucy made it to work with only minutes to spare. Luckily no one was in line at the time clock, and she was able to punch in and then rush down the hall to the store, where she found Hannah closing the drawer of the cash register. She turned and gave Lucy a sunny smile as she ran in.

"Some storm last night, wasn't it?" Hannah remarked as Lucy stashed her bag and umbrella underneath the counter.

"I'm sorry I'm late," Lucy apologized. "I didn't get to sleep until late last night."

"Oh, honey, don't you even worry about it," Hannah said consolingly, "I just got in myself." Lucy knew that was a lie but was grateful all the same. "I spent most of the night in the basement just in case a tornado came while I was asleep," Hannah continued. "You never can tell with storms like that." Lucy nodded her agreement as Hannah handed her the keys to the front door. "Unlock that door for me, dear, and I'll go bring in the bread cart."

Lucy did as she was told. As she turned the key to unlock the door, she glanced out at the storm looming on the horizon. It made a strange picture to be standing in a patch of sunshine surrounded by dark, turbulent thunderclouds. As lightning traced the sky, Lucy tried to conjure up the feeling of Harry's fingers rubbing her own, conjure the weight of his presence as they lay together watching the storm. His kisses had been like a dream, and she wondered if she had been dreaming.

She was so lost in her reverie that she barely noticed the clatter Hannah's bread cart made as she shoved it through the door. Lucy shook off her daydream, unlocked the other door, and then turned to help Hannah with the cart.

Business that morning was brisk. Many shoppers came in to stock up before the storm. Lucy and Hannah managed to keep busy until the storm was right above them. As the last shopper made a break for her car, Lucy and Hannah watched as the sky turned to night and rain began to strike the ground with such force that it actually bounced back up several inches.

"Here comes the wind," Lucy said quietly as the row of saplings that lined the parking lot began to bend to the giant hand of Mother Nature.

"I do believe it's raining sideways," Hannah commented. The two women shared a chuckle that was cut short as a car pulled into the driveway.

"My goodness, I wouldn't want to be driving around in this mess," Hannah remarked as the car made its way around the building to the rear parking lot, where the employees parked. Lucy nodded her agreement. "I wonder who that could be," Hannah said. "That car certainly didn't look familiar."

Lucy shrugged, turning away to tidy up the packages of bread and buns that hadn't been sold that morning. A minute later, Hannah turned to help her, and the two women worked in a companionable silence.

Lucy was spared from reentering her daydream by the telephone. Hannah left her side to answer it. She returned a moment later.

"Dave wants you in his office, Lucy," she said with a small frown. "Everything's all right, isn't it?"

Lucy returned her frown and added a shrug. "As far as I know. Did he say what it was for?"

Hannah shook her head. "No, he just asked me to send you on down the hall." Lucy shrugged again and then hurried out of the store. The hallway was empty, and the door to Dave's office was closed. Lucy walked up and knocked timidly. From within, she heard a cough then a gruff, "Come in." Slowly she opened the door and peered around it.

"Dave?" she began but stopped when she saw a familiar face swiveling around in the chair in front of Dave's desk. "Detective Brown...what are you doing here?" she asked, surprised. Mark Blont stood nearby and gave Lucy a reassuring smile.

Detective Brown got up from the chair and walked over to where Lucy stood, his hand out.

"Came to see you, of course." Detective Brown smiled at her as he shook her hand warmly. "I asked Deputy Blont to let you know I was coming. He did, didn't he?" Mark nodded from the corner.

Lucy mirrored his nod absentmindedly as she looked from Dave to Detective Brown and then back to Dave, who was looking at her oddly. More than anything, she hoped Detective Brown hadn't said anything to Dave about her ghosts, Her worst fears were confirmed by his next words.

"I was just telling Mr. Landerkin about your help with our investigation." Detective Brown gave her hand a last reassuring squeeze and then turned and pointed to the chair next to him.

Lucy took the hint and moved to sit down as Detective Brown took his seat. She fought the urge to squirm as Dave continued to scrutinize her, his expression a mixture of confusion and concern. Detective Brown didn't seem to notice as he went on.

"I tried your house first, thinking you might still be home, but your neighbor told me you were probably here," he said amiably as he searched his jacket pocket. "I brought something for you." Lucy looked down as he passed her an envelope. "Open it," he urged.

Lucy tore open the envelope. She gasped at its contents. "It's a check," she stammered as her hand began to shake.

"For twenty thousand dollars," Detective Brown finished for her. "It's the reward the Martinis offered. When I told them how we were able to locate Shelly...and Jeannie, they wanted you to have it."

Lucy stared at the check, her mouth working soundlessly.

Detective Brown leaned over and looked into her face. "They want to meet you, too."

Lucy suddenly found her voice. "No, no, I can't do that. What would I say to them?" She held out the check and tried to let go of it. "And I can't accept this," she continued. "I don't deserve this money. I really didn't do anything."

Detective Brown refused to take the check and pushed her hand back to her. "Yes, you did do something," he said. "You put yourself on the line for those girls. You risked doubt, ridicule...even a possible arrest to help them. The Martinis understand that, and they are grateful. You gave them their daughter back. You helped us catch her murderers. We found the photos, and they were more incriminating than we could possibly have hoped for." He reached out and took her hand. "You did that, Lucy. You brought those men to justice. You saved at least one woman's life, and who knows how many more. You deserve that money, and you deserve their thanks."

Lucy looked from Detective Brown to Dave, who looked as if he was having a hard time processing the information he was hearing. At her glance, Dave coughed self-consciously, and then he looked down at his desk, as if searching for water. Detective Brown followed her gaze. He coughed himself as he came to the correct conclusion.

"Mr. Landerkin," he began, "I realize how odd all this must seem to you, but please take my word for it—you've got an exceptional young woman here. I'm sure you can understand how much her life is going to change after this gets out."

Startled, Lucy turned and looked at Detective Brown. "Gets out? What do you mean 'gets out'?"

"This is a very big case, Lucy. The media have already picked up on the fact that we had help and that it was rather unorthodox. Just yesterday, one of our local newspaper guys phoned me to follow up on the fact that a psychic helped us solve the case."

Lucy shook her head in denial. "But I'm not a psychic," she protested. "I'm not anything like those people you see on television talking about visions and feelings and stuff."

"That's right," Detective Brown agreed. "You're not anything like those people on the TV because you're real. Those people are just frauds looking for fame or money. But they never really helped anybody. You have."

Lucy looked back down at the check in her hands without really seeing it. More than anything, she wished Harry were there with her. Quietly she murmured his name and hoped he could hear her. A moment later, he appeared, and Lucy felt almost weak with relief. His expression was curious as he knelt next to her and looked at the check in her hands. Then he let out a long, slow whistle.

"My goodness, that's a lot of money. Did Detective Brown bring that?" he asked.

Lucy gave an imperceptible nod. She wasn't comfortable talking to Harry in front of Dave, though she probably would have in front of Detective Brown, given their history together. Instead she tried another tactic.

"Do I have to meet with Shelly's parents on television, or can I just meet them in private?" she asked with mild sarcasm.

"Television?" Harry asked as Detective Brown smiled and shook his head.

"No, I think they'd just like to thank you. That's all."

"Then what about this newspaper guy you mentioned? Can't you just tell him that I don't want to have my name in the papers?"

Harry sat back on his heels as comprehension dawned on his face. "I get it. They want to know how Detective Brown solved his case, don't they?"

Lucy nodded again slightly as Detective Brown appeared to consider her request. Dave, who was clearly confused by it all, looked back and forth between the two of them.

"Well, how about I ask him to leave your name out of the article, though I can't guarantee that he will," he offered.

Lucy nodded, and Detective Brown sighed his satisfaction.

"Well, I've got to catch a flight to DC, though I'm not sure I'll be flying out in this storm," he said. Just then, a boom of thunder shook the room as if confirming his statement. Detective Brown stood up and held out his hand to Dave. "Thanks so much for letting me see Lucy. I won't intrude on you any further." Dave shook his hand wordlessly as he, too, stood up from behind his desk. Then the two men turned to look at Lucy, who paused for a moment, and then they stood up as well.

"Lucy, despite the circumstances, I have to say it's been a pleasure." Detective Brown shook her hand warmly. "I'll give you a call when the Martinis are ready to meet you, OK?"

"OK," Lucy responded hesitantly. Detective Brown smiled at her one last time before letting himself out of the room, with Mark following.

When Lucy turned to follow, Dave called her back with a quiet "Lucy?"

Lucy turned back to see him dropping heavily into his chair. She remained standing and watched as he rubbed his face with his large, beefy hands. Then he dropped them and looked at her tiredly.

"Your friend there told me about your helpin' those girls," he began. He paused, as if uncertain how to continue. "He...uh...mentioned that you could see 'em and talk to 'em, even though they weren't living anymore."

Lucy glanced at Harry, who shrugged, and then she turned back to Dave and nodded slightly. "Yes," she said quietly.

Dave looked around awkwardly as if searching for something on his desk. He settled his gaze on Lucy's feet. "Is it everyone who's dead or just those girls?" he asked after a very long and very awkward moment. When the question was done, he reluctantly met her eyes.

"Just people who are missing...and dead," she answered just as reluctantly. "I mean...the people who I can see and hear are people who have gone missing and have died, but no one knows they've died. I can't see or hear people like my mother or my grandmother or...Mrs. Landerkin." Lucy took a guess at what he was trying to ask her. It was well known that Dave's beloved wife, Jessica, had passed away several years earlier from leukemia.

Dave smiled at that. Then he sighed again. "Why don't you go on back to the shop before Hannah thinks *you've* gone missing." Lucy returned his smile and turned to go.

"Lucy?" Dave called to her yet again, and Lucy turned back. This time he looked concerned. "Be safe...OK?"

Lucy nodded. "I will," she said. She left the office. She was glad to see that Mark had waited for her in the hallway.

"That's great news, right?" Mark asked. His expression looked hopeful.

Lucy smiled. "It is, but there's something else I need to talk to you about."

Mark's expression sobered. "There's something I need to tell you, too. I know that the North Carolina guys feel good about what you did for them, and they don't have any issues with how you came by the information about those two girls, but...well...when I submitted my report, the sheriff took issue with your 'ability' and requested that you be assessed by the department of adult protective services for competency."

Harry scowled as Lucy stood speechless. "What? Why?" she asked.

Mark stared at his feet. "I'm really sorry, Lucy. He's got a real problem with the ghost thing. The county has a social worker and consulting psychiatrist who are going to schedule a visit with you."

Lucy looked bleak. "They think I'm crazy, don't they?" she asked quietly.

"Or lying," Mark replied. "But it doesn't matter. They'll see you're not crazy or lying. It'll be fine." Mark glanced toward the door. "I've got to go. I'm supposed to take Detective Brown to the airport. You'll be OK, right?" he asked, and Lucy nodded. She could tell he felt terrible, so she gave him a reassuring smile she didn't really feel like giving. Then she turned and slowly made her way down the hall.

Rather than go straight to the shop, though, Lucy and Harry stopped by the locker room, which was thankfully empty. Lucy sat down on one of the long benches that ran the length of the room and stared at the check.

"That's a lot of money," Harry said as he sat next to her.

Lucy nodded. "I should probably give it back."

Harry sighed and took one of her hands. "You're not crazy. You didn't cheat anyone. It was given to you because of the help you were able to provide given your unique ability. You came by it honestly, and you are entitled to it."

Lucy shook her head. "But still...it's just too much. And I'm still not sure I'm *not* crazy."

Harry smiled at her and pulled her up off the bench. "How about this idea: you buy a computer with part of it and whatever service you need to be able to use the Internet from home and donate the rest of the money to charity. A crazy person wouldn't do that."

Lucy smiled. "I like that idea," she replied as she folded the check and tucked it into her shirt pocket. "Now, I'd really better get back to Hannah before she sends out the National Guard."

"I'll see you at home," Harry said. He pulled her close and kissed the spot on her cheek just above the edge of her lips. Lucy shivered as he disappeared.

She hurried down the hall, hoping her blush would be gone by the time she reached the store.

# TWENTY

As the storm continued to rage overhead, the store remained deserted. Desperate for some kind of activity, Lucy and Hannah managed to exhaust every possible task until there was nothing left to do but go home. When Dave came in to officially close up the shop, he moved around Lucy, carefully avoiding her. Hannah didn't seem to notice, but Lucy sensed the unease Dave was obviously feeling. It was with relief that she finally fled into the rain to her car. All the way home, she cursed Detective Brown for telling Dave about her ghosts and the sheriff for thinking she was crazy. As she pulled into her driveway, she was relieved to find it empty of the photographers and news vans she had been picturing in her head.

Inside, it was another story. Her home was once again full to the brim with ghosts. Harry sat at the center of it all, taking notes from the newer faces in the crowd. He looked up and smiled as she came in from the rain. Lucy smiled back and accepted a dry towel from Michael, the lost hiker who was next on her list.

"Looks like we have some additions to our happy family," Lucy joked half-heartedly. Michael laughed with her. She dried off her hair and then tossed the towel onto the nearest chair. "I'm going to go change. I'll be right back," she said to Harry, and then she left the room.

When she returned to the kitchen, she found Harry and Michael waiting patiently at the table with Scott in the third chair, looking out of place among the adults. Lucy gave him a reassuring smile as she sat in the fourth chair.

"Are you up to making some phone calls?" Harry asked. Michael looked so hopeful that Lucy could hardly say no.

"Sure," she answered. She picked up the phone.

As luck would have it, Harry had found Michael's name on a website that listed missing persons around the world. Under Michael's picture was a toll-free number that Lucy now dialed. As she listened to the rings, she could see Whitney saunter in, the other ghosts giving her a wide berth. Whitney leaned on the counter across from where Lucy was sitting and crossed her arms, her expression part disdain, part amusement. Lucy ignored her.

The rings ended in a recording that directed callers to please hold...so Lucy held. It was only a few more moments before a human voice came on the line with a curt, "Parker Investigations." Lucy was caught off-guard. Most of her calls had been to either family members or hotlines for local law-enforcement agencies. She stammered at first, coughed, and then finished the script in a rush. The woman on the other end paused for a moment, as if considering the veracity of Lucy's words. Everyone waited expectantly as Whitney smirked.

"Let me see if I got this right," the woman started out slowly. "You're offering information about the disappearance of Michael Huff, am I correct?"

"Yes," Lucy answered firmly.

"And you are saying that he fell while hiking near Smith Peak in the Yosemite National Park," the woman continued slowly, as if she was writing as she was speaking.

"Yes," Lucy said again. She knew what was coming next.

"Can you tell me how you happen to have come by this information?" the woman asked.

Lucy sighed. "Is this part really necessary?" Harry and Michael looked on sympathetically.

"Yes and no." It was the woman's turn to sigh now. "Listen...we get a lot of callers with information about our missing-persons cases. Michael's is no different. And we are obligated to follow up on every possible lead. That said, it's going to be a bitch trying to verify your story, so I would appreciate it if you could at least give me some sort of idea of how you came by this knowledge. Did you know Michael previously?"

"I'm not really comfortable answering a question like that." Lucy said. Before she could continue, though, Harry interrupted.

"Tell her to call Detective Brown," he urged, and Michael nodded. Lucy nodded back.

"What if I give you the name of two men who can verify my...uh... methods," Lucy offered. "After you speak with them, I'll answer any other questions you might have."

The woman on the phone was silent for a minute, and then she sighed, as if giving up. "All right, then, give me their names and numbers, and I'll give them a call."

Lucy gave her Detective Brown's name and number, Mark Blont's name and number, and then added her own number at the end.

"State and local police, huh?" the woman sounded impressed. "Well, I'll give them a call. Depending what I hear from them, I may or may not be calling you back."

"Fair enough," Lucy replied. She said good-bye then hung up the phone.

"That's it?" Whitney sneered. "That's all you do? Great...just great. Well, if anyone needs me, I'll be spending eternity stuck here in Mayberry." No one was disappointed when Whitney stalked out of the room.

Michael shook his head. He looked at Lucy. "Don't mind her. She's the type that no matter what her situation is, she'll make it worse. Very high maintenance." Harry nodded in agreement.

Lucy took a deep breath as she massaged her head. She had thought her headaches had been lessening in intensity lately, but this latest one was a doozy. She briefly entertained the idea of naming them like the weather service named hurricanes. This one she'd definitely name Whitney.

Harry's expression changed as he looked at her closely. Then he leaned over and said something to Michael, who looked at Lucy more closely. Michael then stood up and got a glass of water and Lucy's extra-strength pain relievers. She smiled her thanks, shook out three of the pills, and swallowed them quickly. Harry and Michael looked at each other wordlessly. Then they looked back at Lucy.

"Why don't you go and get some rest," Harry said. Michael nodded his agreement.

Lucy shook her head. "No, I'll be all right. It seems like all I do is sleep anymore. Let's just keep going down the list." She pulled it across the table and picked up the phone. Harry still looked worried but said nothing.

Despite her raging headache, Lucy was still able to make several calls. Though none of the ghosts she called for passed over that night, they all knew that the information that she passed on put them at least a little bit closer. Harry cut it off, though, when Lucy dialed the wrong number three times. She offered only a little protest until Michael and several others joined in, sending her reluctantly out of the room and up to her bedroom, where she changed into a T-shirt and boxer shorts.

She was about to climb into bed when the door opened and a tray floated in, carried by Harry.

"You haven't eaten a thing tonight," he said as he placed the tray at the end of her bed. "Michael thought that might be exacerbating your headache."

Lucy looked over at the bowl of tomato soup and grilled cheese sandwich and grinned. Harry followed her look then grinned back.

"I'm afraid the quality of our fare has fallen since the passing of our dear friend, George," Harry said ruefully.

"Well, beggars can't be choosers," Lucy said with a laugh. "Besides, you'd be surprised how good the food you didn't cook tastes." Then she moved to the end of the bed and sat cross-legged next to the tray. Harry chuckled as she began to eat with relish. They chatted quietly as Lucy ate her dinner. Harry was smiling into her eyes when they heard a snort at the door.

"Well, isn't this cozy," Whitney drawled from the doorway, where she was leaning against the frame.

Lucy covered her mouth with a napkin as she swallowed too quickly. When she looked up, Harry had moved away from her slightly as if embarrassed at having been caught in Lucy's bedroom. The subtle movement was not lost on Whitney, whose smirk only deepened.

"Perhaps no one mentioned it to you, but my bedroom is off-limits," Lucy said curtly.

Whitney put her hands up in mock horror. "Oh dear, have I intruded on your tête-à-tête?" she gasped dramatically. "No one mentioned that your boudoir here was off-limits...to almost everyone. Pardon me." Then she disappeared.

Lucy looked over at Harry, who was frowning at the now-empty tray. She was incensed that Whitney had managed to ruin their warm, pleasant moment. She wanted to say something nasty about Whitney but couldn't bring herself to do so. Instead she watched silently as Harry picked up the tray and carried it to the door, where he turned back.

"Try to get some sleep," he urged quietly. He left, closing the door behind him.

Lucy stared at the door forlornly. She pulled her legs up against her chest and rested her chin on her knees. She closed her eyes, willed Harry to come back, and then opened them again, but she saw...nothing. Dispirited, she fell back to lie on the bed, her legs still clutched to her chest. The ache in her head was nothing compared to the ache that was growing in her heart. Her last thought before she fell asleep was a curse for Whitney.

# TWENTY-ONE

The next morning, the phone woke Lucy up. Her eyes barely open, she glanced at the clock and saw that it was only six. With a groan, she pushed herself up and then stumbled to the hallway to answer the phone that sat on a small table.

"Hello?" she mumbled.

"Lucy? This is Mark. I'm so sorry about calling so early, but I wanted to warn you that the social worker and psychiatrist are going to make a surprise visit this morning. I'm not supposed to tell you, but I don't think it's fair that they want to come unannounced."

"But I have work," Lucy objected.

"I called Dave and let him know that you might be a little bit late. I didn't tell him why, though. I made it sound like we just have a follow-up meeting. He said it was fine if you went in when you're done. I'm sorry about the time. I just wanted you to have enough time to...get it together, I guess."

"OK," Lucy said with a sigh. "Thank you."

"No problem," Mark replied. "I'll try and follow up with you later."

Lucy said good-bye and hung up. She wasn't surprised when Harry appeared next to her.

"You heard?" she asked him. Harry nodded.

"I guess I'll go take a shower," she said quietly, and she turned and walked back into her room.

When she came out from her shower, Lucy found Harry seated on her bed. His expression was a combination of concern and sadness.

Lucy pulled her towel tighter around herself and sat down next to him. "You look like someone just died," she joked lamely.

Harry gave her a reluctant smile and then put his arm around her and pulled her close. She thought about how he felt solid, like a living human being, losing herself in his warmth.

"I feel thoroughly responsible for your predicament," he mourned. "If I hadn't found you, or if I'd just left you alone, you wouldn't be faced with such terrible accusations."

Lucy felt her deepest fear come forth. "What if I am crazy?" she asked quietly. "What if you don't really exist...or you exist, but only in my head?"

"Then I'm glad I'm here," Harry replied as quietly. "If I exist only in your head, then I'm glad your head conjured me. I wouldn't want to be anywhere else."

Lucy's heart swelled with his words. She didn't want to say anything that would ruin the moment, so she sank further into his embrace and closed her eyes.

They sat that way in silence, as if both were hesitant to start the day. Lucy knew she needed to at least be dressed when the social worker arrived, so she reluctantly pulled from Harry's embrace and went to get dressed.

Downstairs, there was a surprising dearth of ghosts. Only Michael and a handful of other ghosts lingered in the kitchen. Whitney was nowhere to be seen.

Lucy accepted a mug of coffee from Michael with thanks and then sat at the table with Harry. It was still too early for a visit, but she wasn't surprised when someone knocked at the door. As a unit, all the ghosts turned to look at the front door with concern.

Lucy sighed and got up to answer it.

On her front step was an older-looking couple. If she didn't know better, Lucy would have thought they were Jehovah's Witnesses or Mormons coming to spread the word. Both looked to be somewhere in their late forties or early fifties and were dressed as if they were going to church. The woman was heavyset with a kind face and faded brown hair threaded with gray, while the man looked like everyone's boring, normal dad or a middle-school principal. He was also on the heavy side, and what hair he had left might have been brown at one time. Watery blue eyes swam behind thick, wire-framed glasses, completing his everyman look.

"Lucy Godwin?" the woman asked. Lucy nodded. "I'm Barbara Williamson, and this is Dr. John Dawson. We're with the Department of Job and Family Services. May we come in?"

Lucy nodded again and opened the door wide for them to enter. She could tell as they stepped into the house that they were making note of everything, from the worn furniture to the faded photos hanging on the walls. She was grateful that the house was clean, at least.

"Can I offer you some coffee or tea, maybe?" Lucy offered as they sat down.

"No, thank you," Mrs. Williamson answered, pulling out a file folder. "We won't take up too much of your time." Lucy took the last seat in her small, shabby living room. Harry moved next to her and placed a reassuring hand on her shoulder.

Fortified by his presence, Lucy asked, "Can I ask why you're here, then?"

"We were notified by the sheriff's department that you might be experiencing some...issues that may affect your ability to function independently," Mrs. Williamson said carefully. Dr. Dawson nodded soberly next to her.

"And why would they notify you?"

Mrs. Williamson ignored Lucy's question. "It would be our responsibility to make that determination and then recommend a next step...if it's appropriate. We just want to ask you some questions. I promise this won't take long."

Lucy doubted that but nodded. "Fine," she answered.

Mrs. Williamson seemed satisfied and pulled a form out from her folder, while Dr. Dawson grabbed a pen from his shirt pocket and opened his own file. They had no idea that the room was filling with ghosts curious about who they were and what they were doing. Whitney was the last one in and had a bemused smile on her face.

"So how long have you lived here?"

Lucy looked back at Mrs. Williamson, realizing she'd been watching the ghosts. "Since I was eight." She watched as Mrs. Williamson made a note of her answer.

"And do you live alone?"

Lucy nodded. "Yes."

"Do you have any family?"

Lucy shook her head. "No. My mother died when I was eight, and I came here to live with my grandmother and my aunt. I was thirteen when my grandmother died and twenty-one when my aunt died. She left me the house."

Mrs. Williamson made a few more notes. "And what about your father?"

Lucy shrugged. "He died before I was born...overseas."

Mrs. Williamson looked up. "Overseas?"

"He was in the army. When he left for his deployment, he and my mom didn't know she was pregnant. He was killed at a roadside checkpoint just after arriving."

Lucy squirmed as everyone in the room, ghosts included, looked at her with sympathy. She tried to ignore Dr. Dawson as he made notations on the paper in front of him.

"So your mother raised you alone?"

Lucy nodded. "Until she died."

"And how did she die?"

Lucy paused. "She committed suicide," she answered quietly.

That gave Mrs. Williamson pause. "I'm so sorry," she said. "What was she like?"

"Sad," Lucy answered. "Beautiful and kind and very, very sad."

"Because of your father?"

Lucy nodded. "Yes," she answered simply, leaving it at that. Her mother was none of their business.

"And what was your grandmother like...and your aunt? Did you have a good relationship with them?"

Lucy nodded again. She was beginning to feel like a bobblehead. "They were wonderful. Very loving...very protective."

"It must be hard not having any family," Mrs. Williams stated. Lucy wondered if Dr. Dawson was going to say anything.

"It's not great sometimes, but...I'm used to it. My grandmother and aunt were very active in the community. I don't know where you're from, but people take care of each other here. They don't judge."

Mrs. Williamson put down her pen. "I hope you don't feel like we're judging you, Lucy."

Lucy tilted her head. "Isn't that exactly what you're doing? Judging me?"

"I know it's hard to understand, but we're only here to make sure you are safe. Why don't we just finish with our questions?" It didn't escape Lucy's notice that Mrs. Williamson didn't answer her question.

"I understand that you work?" she asked, and Lucy nodded again.

"Where do you work?"

"Landerkin Bakery."

"And how long have you worked there?"

"Almost seven years."

"What do you do there?"

Lucy sighed. "I used to work on the packaging line, but now I work in the bakery store."

"Have you had any problems at work recently?"

Lucy shook her head. "No."

"And how about with your friends or boyfriends...any trouble there?"

Lucy paused. She knew she should admit to her fight with Jerry but didn't want to give Mrs. Williamson, or Dr. Dawson, any more information than was absolutely necessary.

"Not really," was the best answer she could come up with. Luckily, Mrs. Williamson didn't seem to notice the ambiguity of her reply.

"I want to ask you about the statement Deputy Blont made in his report regarding the means by which you acquired the information about the missing girls," Mrs. Williamson said. She looked at Lucy pointedly.

Lucy did not want to make Mrs. Williamson's job any easier, so she returned the gaze without answering. The two women stared at each other impassively for a very long minute until Dr. Dawson's discomfort moved him to speak.

"I'd like to ask you some questions about that, if I may," he intoned. His voice was deep and melodious, like a late-night radio DJ.

But Lucy wasn't giving him an inch, either. She turned and stared at him.

To his credit, he appeared to be unperturbed by her lack of response, so he continued without preamble.

"I understand that the information about the missing girls came to you from their spirits...their ghosts?" he asked.

Lucy wasn't sure how to answer that. If she lied and denied her ability to see and hear ghosts, then she would lose all her credibility. But if she admitted her ability, her credibility would be in question anyway. It really was a lose/lose situation for her.

"Yes," she answered simply.

"Can you see them?" he asked. "Are they visible to you?"

"Yes."

"How do they appear to you?"

Lucy wondered if this was a trick question. "I see them like I see you, but they're not quite all there. They're a little bit see-through."

"And do you see them all the time? Or just at certain times of the day...like early in the morning?"

"I see them all the time."

Dr. Dawson made a note on his own paperwork. "And how do you speak with them? How do you hear them?"

Lucy was confused by the question. "They talk to me, and I talk to them...I guess. I never really thought about that."

"Let me ask it this way...how do they communicate with you?"

"They just say things out loud like you are right now."

"I apologize if this seems complicated to consider, but do you hear them the way you're hearing me? Or do you hear them in your head... psychically?"

"I just...hear them."

"Do you see them now?" he asked, and Lucy nodded. "What would happen if they spoke right now? Would we be able to hear them? Would they talk to us?"

Whitney smirked. She walked over and put her lips near Dr. Dawson's ear. "You are a fat fucking fuck," she said loud enough for the ghosts all the way in the kitchen to chuckle in response.

Lucy tried not to smile.

"Did they say something?" Dr. Dawson asked.

"One of them said you could stand to lose a little weight," Lucy paraphrased, and the ghosts collectively laughed.

Dr. Dawson grunted and sat back to make another notation.

"What kinds of things do they say to you? What do they tell you?"

Lucy paused and wondered where Dr. Dawson was going with his question. "He thinks you may be schizophrenic," Harry murmured next to her, and the ghosts shifted angrily.

"We have normal conversations like you and I are having right now." Lucy answered.

"Do they tell you to do things...like harm yourself or others?"

Lucy was indignant. "Of course not. They ask for help or give me information about themselves." Lucy felt the room get colder as the ghosts grew angrier. Dr. Dawson didn't seem to notice the change, though Mrs. Williamson pulled her cardigan closer around her.

"What is your physical health like?" he continued.

"Fine. I get headaches now and then, but otherwise I think I'm healthy."

Dr. Dawson looked at her more closely. "What kind of headaches?"

"Just headaches," Lucy answered. "I've always had a problem with headaches."

"Are they severe or mild?"

Lucy shrugged. "They're severe when there's a lot going on, which has been pretty much all the time lately." Harry looked at her and squeezed her hand in sympathy.

"And are they localized or all over?"

"They're always on the right side...like behind my right eye, if that's what you're asking."

Lucy watched him make some more notes.

"Have you seen a doctor about your headaches?" he asked. "Or had any tests to determine why you might be getting them?"

Lucy shook her head. "No. I just take some ibuprofen and take a nap. They don't get in the way of anything; they're just an inconvenience."

Dr. Dawson sat quietly and made more notations, so Mrs. Williamson picked up the interview questions. Though she'd seemed nice, or at least polite when they first came in, her demeanor had changed considerably.

"Deputy Blont indicated in his report that you were able to verify the presence of these so-called spirits when they 'broke a tape recorder' in front of the investigators," she stated flatly. Lucy could tell she thought either Mark was lying or Lucy was.

"Is that a question?" Lucy asked, annoyed.

"Can you do that again?" she asked, but her tone was more skeptical than inquisitive.

"I wasn't the one who did it; they were," Lucy answered. "Are you asking for proof of their existence?"

Mrs. Williamson tilted her head and regarded Lucy, adopting a tone that sounded suspiciously sarcastic. "That would go a long way toward helping us understand how you were able to convince several police officers that you're psychic."

"What do you want them to do?"

"Deputy Blont's report said you could accurately report about a photograph and you caused their tape recorder to fail."

"Again, I didn't do any of that. They did."

"Can you ask them to do it again?"

"They can hear you. You need to tell them what you want them to do."

Whitney shook her head in disgust. "This woman is annoying."

Mrs. Williamson appeared to consider her options. "I have a magnet on my refrigerator from my vacation last year. Have them tell me where it's from."

Lucy tried to keep her irritation from her voice. "Like me, they aren't psychic. You need to tell them where you live."

Mrs. Williamson smirked but remained silent, while Dr. Dawson shifted uncomfortably.

"Whitney, if you sit inside of her you might be able to discern her address. She's probably thinking it right now," Harry said.

Whitney gave Mrs. Williamson her own smirk, which was far more effective as expressions go, and moved over to sit in the other woman. Mrs. Williamson jerked and sat up straight, as if an electrical current ran through her. A second later, Whitney moved away. She disappeared as Mrs. Williamson slumped over, her teeth chattering.

"Wha...at was tha...t?" she said through her teeth.

"That's how they find information about you," Lucy answered.

Whitney appeared a moment later. "God, that woman's house is a mess. She's got shit stacked floor to ceiling. Shopping bags everywhere."

Lucy started reciting Whitney's words. "It's like you're the Home Shopping Network's biggest fan. How much crap jewelry do you really need? Anyway, the magnet's from the Liberace Museum. Who even knew that existed? It's made out of some sort of plastic, and it's a grand piano covered in fake crystals. Super tacky." Lucy watched as Mrs. Williamson's face first went pale and then turned red with embarrassment. "Whitney can be a little blunt," Lucy said a little more kindly.

"And what about the tape recorder?" Mrs. Williamson asked in an attempt to turn the interview back to Lucy. "How did you do that?"

Whitney bent over and flicked Mrs. Williamson's pen so hard it flew straight at her and struck her in the center of her forehead, leaving a faint blue streak. It fell into her lap.

Both Mrs. Williamson and Dr. Dawson sat staring at the pen, their expressions of shock identical. Then Mrs. Williamson seemed to remember herself.

"You did that somehow," she said, grabbing at her papers and her bag. She stood up, letting the offending pen fall to the floor, and stepped away from it as if it were contaminated somehow. Dr. Dawson followed suit ponderously.

"I don't know how you did it, and I don't care," Mrs. Williamson continued. "You can keep you 'psychic' nonsense and your ghosts. You're not my problem."

Mrs. Williamson moved toward the front door. She stopped short as it opened, seemingly of its own volition. She couldn't know that one of the other ghosts stood next to it with his hand on the knob.

She let out an involuntary squeak and fled the house.

Lucy turned and saw Dr. Dawson holding out a business card. "That was very interesting. However, I'm concerned about the headaches. I suggest you make an appointment with your personal physician. And you are always welcome to give me a call."

Lucy took the card and stared at it as Dr. Dawson followed Mrs. Williamson out. The door slammed behind them, and the ghosts collectively chucked as Whitney congratulated herself on her performance.

"Somehow I don't think we'll be bothered by them again," Harry mused.

Lucy shook her head, tossing Dr. Dawson's card into the wastebasket. "Me, neither," she answered. "Now I've got to get to work."

# TWENTY-TWO

In the wee hours of the next morning, Lucy awoke to a babbling of voices. With an odd sense of déjà vu, she sat up in bed and listened closely. The noise of the voices crested and then ebbed, as if an ocean of people stood just outside her door. It was still dark outside, so she assumed she hadn't been asleep for very long, but a glance at her bedside clock told her that it was almost five o'clock in the morning. Now fully awake, Lucy threw a pair of sweatpants over her boxer shorts. She opened the door and stuck her head out into the hallway.

Since she had begun helping her ghostly visitors, they had all come to an unspoken agreement to allow Lucy to live as normal a life as possible, which meant that her bedroom was sacrosanct, as well as her rest. Lucy slept undisturbed unless it was for something urgent. Even then, someone, usually Harry, would come and wake her. But this was different. The voices sounded different...crisp, and businesslike, a buzzing of bees swarming over their hive. As Lucy padded quietly down the stairs, she realized that the voices were coming not from inside, but from outside. Downstairs, she looked around and found the living room empty, which was strange. Usually at least three or four of the newly missing stayed nearby, either out of a need to maintain some sort of normalcy or simply for the comfort of a home, even if it was not theirs.

Lucy turned back to the window next to the front door. For some reason, she stayed to the side and peeked out without moving the curtains. What she saw made her stomach drop—out on her meager front yard were several news vans with freshly pressed and expertly coiffed reporters speaking urgently into microphones. The lights from the news cameras were blinding as they illuminated every inch of the front of her modest little home.

Lucy turned away from the window and chewed on the side of her thumb as she wondered what to do. She desperately wanted to call out for Harry, but the cruelty of Whitney's comments had driven a wedge of embarrassment between them. Softly, she called out the next name that popped into her head—and then cursed the fact that Mark could not appear the same way Harry could.

Then, as if in answer to her prayer, Lucy heard the whoop of a siren just outside her door. She peeked again and saw both Mark and Deputy Acco getting out of two patrol cars that were now pulled up onto her front lawn. Mark went up to the news reporters as Deputy Acco made his way across the lawn to her front door. Lucy opened it and let him in before he could even knock.

"You heard?" he asked grimly as she quickly shut the door behind him.

"No...I mean, I heard the voices outside, but I don't know why they're there," Lucy answered.

Deputy Acco took off his uniform cap that was now covered in bright yellow plastic to protect it from the rain that continued to fall. Lucy took it and his yellow slicker and hung them on the rack next to the door.

"Well, from what we've been able to gather, someone leaked the story of your helping the North Carolina guys to the press. Your neighbor next door called us when the news vans started pulling into her driveway." Deputy Acco took out a clean white handkerchief and wiped off the fine mist of rain that had settled on his face. "Mark and I just now managed to clear out the end of the street so we could get here," he continued. "Mark's going to try to push them back as much as possible till we can figure out exactly how to handle this."

Lucy peeked out again and saw that two other deputies had joined Mark in his efforts. Then she sighed and went into the kitchen to make coffee for everyone. Deputy Acco joined her and silently began to help.

It was fully light, and the house was rapidly filling with ghosts, though Harry was not among them, when Mark was finally able to come in. He removed his hat and coat, hung them next to Deputy Acco's, and then joined them in the kitchen, where he gratefully accepted a cup of coffee. Without a word, Deputy Acco got up, donned his now-dry cap and coat, and went out into the rain.

Lucy looked on bleakly as Mark gulped down his coffee in an attempt to warm up.

"Any idea what they want?" Lucy asked.

Mark gave her a wry smile. "They want to talk to the woman who can talk to the dead," he joked. "That's what they want."

Lucy had no answer for that, so she said nothing, choosing to pour another cup of coffee for Mark, who accepted gratefully. As she was pouring coffee for the deputies outside, Michael appeared at her shoulder.

"Harry sent me to tell you that he would be here soon," he said quickly. "He's trying to find out how they all found out." Michael jerked his head toward the front door. He smiled wanly. Lucy nodded silently and looked around for a tray Mark could use to take the coffee outside.

Michael sat down at the table, and the two men watched as Lucy loaded up the tray with coffee, doughnuts, and napkins. Mark took one last gulp of coffee and then went into the living room and put on his hat and raincoat. Lucy followed him with the tray and handed it to him before opening the door. Careful to stay out of sight, she was still blinded by the flash of the cameras that began going off the moment the door was opened. Quickly she shut it behind Mark. Then she returned to the kitchen, where she found Harry speaking to Michael.

Her heart warmed at the smile he gave her as she walked in. He sat down with her at the kitchen table. After a moment's hesitation, he took her hands in his.

"Quite a morning it's been," he said wryly, and Lucy smiled back. "I've been flying about, trying to find out how this all happened, and it appears to have all hit the fan at once."

"What do you mean?" Lucy asked.

Harry sighed and squeezed her hand. "Well, Detective Brown's newspaper friend mentioned your story to his friend, who just happens to work at CNN. At the same time, Shelly's parents held a press conference in Virginia, which also was picked up by CNN. Then to top it all off, Ms. Parker, the woman you spoke to yesterday, phoned her local journalist friend, who sent the story of a young psychic out on the Associated Press wire. Now it appears that several of the families you contacted have also phoned CNN to tell their side of the story. One of them just happens to be a Mrs. Cherise Miglione."

"Great," Lucy mumbled. She pressed the heels of her hands against her eyes. "Now what do I do?"

"You get a spokesperson," Whitney said crisply from the doorway. "You appoint someone, your lawyer or a family friend, to speak on your behalf. Make it someone who can field all the embarrassing questions the press is going to throw your way."

Lucy shook her head and said, "I don't have a lawyer or family... and unfortunately, no one can see my friends." This she said with a wry smile.

Whitney rolled her eyes at the ceiling. "Don't you know *anyone* who isn't dead?"

Lucy shook her head again. "No one that I trust enough," she began. Then she paused, considering, "unless I ask Mark to speak for me."

"Ugh, the cop?" Whitney replied with her hands on her hips. "Well, if that's the best you can do, you'd better get him in here to help you prepare a statement."

Lucy looked at Whitney with distrust, despite the soundness of her advice. "Why do I have to make a statement? Couldn't I just say 'no comment' and wait for them to go away?"

Whitney gave Lucy an indulgent yet insincere smile. "You don't know much about the press, do you?" Then she sighed and moved over to the table to take the last chair. "There are three ways of responding to the press. The first is to make no statement at all and hope they get tired of waiting. The problem with that tactic is that it leads to a great deal of speculation and leaves the door wide open for anyone who knows you even a little bit to publicly comment. You don't want that." Lucy had to agree, and Whitney nodded with satisfaction.

"The second approach is to deny everything, which cuts your part short, but you let down everyone who's come forward with your story, and you come off as potentially unreliable to the families you are trying to help, like a publicity seeker who's gotten in over her head. Not good either, right?" she asked, and Lucy nodded.

185

"So, that leaves you with option number three," Whitney finished.

"Which is?" Lucy prompted.

"Own it all." Whitney held out her hands and shrugged, momentarily shedding her smart-ass persona. "Tell the truth...about everything...and let them sort it out. But when I say the truth, I mean a limited truth. Don't tell them your life story. Just give them the basics, like how you can see us and that you're trying to help us 'pass over' or whatever. Stay low-key, and let the families you've helped vouch for you with their side of the story. The important thing is to not hide anything, though. If you've got any skeletons, the press is going to find them." Whitney looked Lucy up and down, and then she looked around the tiny kitchen. "Somehow I don't think that's going to be a problem, though. You're just too boring to have skeletons."

Lucy ignored that comment, choosing instead to rub the spot over her eye that hurt the most. "So I guess we wait for Mark to come back in."

"Let me see if I can help with that." Michael grinned and disappeared. Lucy looked at Harry, who shrugged. Then the two got up and walked to the window, followed closely by Whitney.

Outside, Lucy could see several of the deputies lining the front of her yard, trying to keep the press at bay. In the center was Mark, who was simultaneously pushing back a photographer and talking into his radio. Michael went up to him and tugged at his sleeve. Mark looked back. He jumped a little when he realized that no one was there. Michael reached out, took Mark's arm, and gently pulled him toward the house. Luckily, Mark understood and with surprising calm turned to follow.

Lucy watched as the remaining deputies closed ranks behind him. She moved aside as he opened the door and stepped onto the towel someone had considerately laid across the threshold.

"Can't say I'm gonna be able to get used to that," Mark said with a sheepish smile, "but I'm glad you didn't try to come outside. What's up?"

"Whitney says I need to appoint a spokesperson to talk to the press. Would you be willing to do that for me?" Lucy asked nervously.

"Who's Whitney?" Mark asked suspiciously, "and how does she know what you should do?"

Lucy ignored Whitney, who snorted behind her. "She's a publicist who was mugged in New York. She sounds like she knows what she's talking about. I think we should listen to her."

Mark scratched the stubble on his chin and considered Lucy's request. "All right," he said finally. "Have your friend Whitney help you write up a statement, and I'll pitch it for you."

Lucy turned quickly and went into the kitchen, where Harry already had a paper and pen waiting. It took only minutes for Whitney to come up with something that would appease the press without giving too much away. Lucy wrote it all out and then ran back to the front door. Mark was still peeking out the window.

"Well, at least no more have shown up," he said as Lucy handed him her statement. "Hopefully this will be enough for them." He read through it quickly and then nodded. "This sounds good. You might want to consider letting them interview you, though. That's what they really want...to talk to you."

"We'll see," Lucy said enigmatically.

Mark put the statement inside his jacket to keep it dry, and then he went out to face the press. Lucy quickly shut the door behind him and turned to Whitney.

"So...what do we do now?" she asked.

"We wait," Whitney replied, turning away.

Waiting turned out to be easier said than done. Lucy found herself pacing the floors as the rain stopped and dawn cast its teary light over the world. Harry and the others sat and watched her pause every so often to peek around the curtain. Whitney got tired of watching her and disappeared for a while, only to reappear during one of Lucy's longer pauses.

"What are you doing?" she asked as Lucy tried to listen to Mark by pressing her ear against the solid wood door.

"I think Mark is reading my statement," Lucy replied. "But I can't quite hear him."

Whitney rolled her eyes skyward and shook her head. "Then turn on the television," she said slowly as if they were all under the age of three.

Lucy stood up and smacked herself on the head for being so simple. She walked over and turned on the ancient console television. Luckily, her meager pay stretched far enough for her to get cable, so she immediately switched to CNN, where she found Mark in the middle of her screen, addressing the assorted journalists with surprising ease, as if he'd been in front of the cameras his whole life. She was chagrined, however, to realize how desperately the front of her house needed to be painted. It appeared that he had finished reading her statement and was fielding questions. Under his picture ran a description of the events as they had been unfolding. It was as Harry had said; the Martinis had spoken with the press about the help she had given them. Then the private investigator looking for Michael had called, as well as George's wife, Cherise. Even Mrs. Bissell, the mother of Melvin, Lucy's first successful contact, gave an interview to reporters.

Lucy pulled her eyes away from the ticker to pay closer attention to the questions the reporters were throwing at Mark. She was not surprised to hear the skepticism in their voices but was caught off-guard by their eagerness to debunk her.

"We've learned that Miss Godwin has been assessed by a psychiatrist. Does Miss Godwin have any history of mental illness, any possible hospitalizations? Is she on any medication?" she heard one of the reporters ask off-camera. Mark had started to shake his head before the reporter had even finished her question and answered immediately.

"No," he declared emphatically. "Miss Godwin has no history of mental illness. She has never been treated for any mental illness, nor is she under any medication." Lucy was reassured by the confidence in Mark's answer.

"Is there any reason to suspect that Miss Godwin might be making false statements about psychic ability to gain some publicity?" another reporter asked.

Again Mark shook his head emphatically. "There is no evidence to suggest that any of the statements Miss Godwin has made have been false. I can state with certainty that every piece of information she has given has been accurate and so highly detailed as to confirm her ability to communicate with the victims."

"It is rumored that the California State Police have requested that Miss Godwin submit to a lie-detector test in the case of missing hiker Michael Huff. Will you comment on that?"

"What?" Lucy cried. "I'm not going to take a lie-detector test!"

"Relax," Whitney said. "They're making it up to rattle you. Anything that begins with 'It is rumored' has a sixty percent chance of being entirely false. They just do that to prolong the news story. Unfortunately, it can create the likelihood of some idiot cop in California thinking he's supposed to drag you in for questioning just because he saw it on television."

Lucy sighed. "Great, just great."

"Any rumor that Miss Godwin's presence has been requested by the California State Police or any other jurisdiction is entirely false. She has been a proven source of reliable information and nothing more. Any other questions based on rumors will be investigated thoroughly to determine the source of those rumors," Mark replied sternly. Then he quickly concluded the impromptu press conference. They watched as Mark turned to cross the small patch of grass and let himself in through the front door. It was surreal to see him simultaneously leave the television screen and enter the house.

"Well done," Whitney said admiringly. "That should put a stop to any more bullshit."

Lucy looked up at Mark as he quickly closed the door behind him. "Whitney thinks you did well," she said as he hung up his coat and hat and walked over to sit with her on the sofa.

"Just doin' my job, ma'am," he drawled. He watched soberly as a reporter's face replaced his on the screen. "They're not giving you much of a break, are they?" he observed as the reporter rehashed the more skeptical questions that were being raised.

The telephone saved Lucy from answering his question. She was about to answer it when Mark put out his hand.

"Let me. It could be another reporter."

Lucy handed him the telephone, and Mark answered it with a curt hello and then smiled as an excited chattering came over the line.

"Here. It's Hannah from the bakery," he said with a laugh, giving the phone back to Lucy.

"Oh my goodness, Lucy, you're famous!" Hannah said breathlessly. "Charles turned on the TV, and what did we hear but those reporters talking about our very own Lucy! And Mark Blont looked so professional giving that press conference. Why, I just about died when they said you were a psychic!"

"But I'm not..." Lucy began, but Hannah went on.

"And how you helped those girls...well, it brought a tear to my eye, it did, when they showed that Shelly girl's mother crying because she finally knew what happened to her daughter. And they had nothing but good things to say about you. But I didn't like that Parker woman at all. She made it sound like you were just trying to get on the TV by saying you could talk to ghosts. I want to give her a piece of my mind, that's for sure. You tell that hiker boy to tell his parents not to pay her a dime. I don't think she even tried to find him. Oh, look. There's your house again."

With the phone still to her ear, Lucy looked at the television and saw that indeed her house was on again, and this time a familiar figure was making his way up to her front door where Mark let him in.

"Well, I didn't get far," Detective Brown joked as he shook Mark's hand.

"Lucy, I need to call Dave and see what he wants us to do. This is just so exciting!" Hannah said. She hung up. Lucy hung up too and went over to take Detective Brown's outstretched hand.

"Must be a slow news day," he joked as he shook her hand warmly. "How are you holding up?"

Lucy shrugged. "As well as can be expected, I guess, though I don't know how I'm going to get to work."

"Well, it's been my experience that they're not going to let up until they hear from you, and we're past the point of being able to avoid them," Detective Brown answered ruefully.

"He's right," Whitney chimed in. "You'll need to give them something to get them off your back."

Lucy sighed. "Fine, then. Let them ask their questions, but they'd better be quick about it. I have to be at work at nine."

Everyone laughed at that, and Detective Brown and Mark put their heads together to come up with a plan. They spoke for a few minutes, deciding it would be best if Lucy answered just a few questions. Then Mark and Deputy Acco would escort her to the bakery, where one of them would stay and try to keep the press from interfering with the other employees. Lucy gave her approval to the plan, so Mark and Detective Brown went out to brief the press.

While he was gone, Hannah called back to say that Dave wanted Lucy at the bakery, where he could keep an eye on her. Lucy began to protest that the news vans would just follow her there, but Hannah cut her off.

"Lucy, honey, Dave's just worried that they'll keep pestering you while you're at home. At least at the bakery you'll have room to move around and things to keep you occupied. He also wants you to bring Mark Blont with you just in case. All right?"

"All right," Lucy answered. "I'll be there...somehow. But they're saying I need to answer some questions first, so I'll come in as soon as that's done."

"That's fine, honey. We'll see you there." Hannah said good-bye and hung up.

"I'll come, too," Harry said quietly. Lucy felt as if an enormous weight had fallen from her.

"Thanks," she whispered.

She went upstairs to get ready for work. When she returned to the living room thirty minutes later, she found Mark and Deputy Acco, as well as all her ghosts, watching the events surrounding her newfound notoriety unfolding on the news. They were now tuned into the local news channel that had managed to dig up some background information on Lucy. Luckily, it was as Whitney had predicted, Lucy was just too boring to have much to report about. Unfortunately, they had unearthed Lucy's yearbook photo, which was now plastered across the TV screen.

"Ugh, could they have found a worse picture?" Lucy groused as she accepted the coffee and slice of toast that Michael had brought in from the kitchen.

"No kidding," Whitney smirked. "You might want to offer them something a little more flattering. Then again...maybe not. That doesn't even look like you. You can breeze right by them, and they won't even know it." Lucy shot her a dirty look. Whitney shrugged. "Just trying to help. At any rate, you need to prepare yourself. They're not out there as your fan club. They'll ask you the same questions they asked your friend, Mark, there. Sure, they'll start out sounding impartial but, you'll see, they'll try to discredit you as quickly as you can say 'sound bite.'" For once, Whitney sounded as if she actually cared.

Lucy sighed. "Let's just get this over with."

Harry moved over and took Lucy's elbow as Mark and Deputy Acco moved in front of her. Then Mark opened the door, and a flurry of cameras and microphones turned in their direction.

Lucy followed them outside, grateful to have Harry by her side. As a group, they crossed the tiny lawn and stopped at a mark on the sidewalk, where Detective Brown waited. He'd briefed the assembled journalists and gave them a warning that they were not to crowd her.

Lucy was nervous as she faced the microphones and cameras. Instantly the reporters began firing questions at her—so many that it was impossible to single one out to answer. Her head was starting to spin when both Mark and Detective Brown put up their hands for silence. Quiet, the teeming throng looked more like a small group of skeptics, each ready to be the one to blow a hole in Lucy's story. Mark addressed the group, firmly asking for some sort of order. They complied and, one by one, began to ask their questions.

Whitney had been right that they would start out with simple questions into her background and early history with the ghosts. One reporter in particular, Lucy noticed, remained silent at first, preferring to document her answers to the others' questions. She had begun to relax when he threw out his first volley.

"Brian Mifflin from the *New York Post*. Miss Godwin, would the twenty-thousand-dollar reward you received from the Martini family be part of your motivation to get involved in these high-profile cases?" he asked with a slight sneer that reminded her of Whitney. She was about to answer in kind when Detective Brown stepped in front of her.

"I arranged for Miss Godwin to receive the full amount of the reward the Martinis offered. It was through her sacrifice that we were able to find Shelly Martini and Jeannie Allen and bring their murderers to justice." Detective Brown spoke with a firmness that Lucy hoped would put an end to Mr. Mifflin's questions. Her hopes were in vain, however, when he shouted over the voices of the other reporters.

"What do you intend to do with the money, and will you be pursuing the rewards offered in the other cases you've involved yourself in?"

"I'd like to buy a computer with part of it, and the rest will go to the Center for Missing and Exploited Children," Lucy answered. Then she turned away to answer a question from another reporter.

Unfortunately, the others had taken up his line of questioning and began to throw out questions about her motives and the truth about her abilities. Lucy began to shake her head in the face of such onslaught. Mark threw his arm out and turned toward Lucy, giving the reporters his back. Detective Brown took over the press conference as Mark and Deputy Acco guided Lucy to the nearest patrol car. She kept her head down the whole way, venturing a look only as she was climbing into the car.

All of her neighbors were outside, held in thrall by the media circus. Mrs. Kelly from next door gave Lucy an encouraging smile and a thumbs up as her daughter stood next to her, waving. Lucy returned the smile and the wave faintly, and then she slouched down in the seat as Mark drove away. Harry took her hand and held it tightly as they rode to the bakery, where thankfully no one waited to ambush them.

Mark parked in the fire lane next to the rear door and rushed Lucy into the building. Once inside the door, they all breathed a sigh of relief. Lucy especially felt safe in the bakery as if it were a fragrant fortress that would protect her from all the doubt and innuendo outside. The door had no sooner closed behind them when Dave opened the office door and stuck his head out.

"You all right there, Lucy?" he asked with great concern that made Lucy feel even better.

"I'm all right," she sighed gratefully. Dave reached over and patted her shoulder awkwardly. He then waved Mark into his office. "Go on and see Hannah, Lucy. The two of you can figure out what you wanna do today."

Lucy nodded as she punched in on the time clock. Then she and Harry went down the hall and into the store, where Hannah was waiting.

"Oh, honey, you looked so lovely on the television!" Hannah cried. Then she drew Lucy into a big, squishy hug before holding her out at arm's length. Her expression turned dark. "I didn't like that *New York Post* guy one bit, though. Thinks he can turn people against you. I'd like to give him a piece of my mind. I'd tell that little shit where he can go. Yes, I would." Lucy gave her a crooked smile and hoped for Brian Mifflin's sake he'd stay away from Hannah.

"Well, what do you think we should do with our field trip today?" Hannah asked as her face cleared. "We've got twenty-five second-grad-ers coming. Dave thought you'd like to take them around, and I'll stay here in the store. That way, if any of those reporters show up, they won't be able to see you from the road."

Lucy looked at Harry, who shrugged and then nodded. "Sounds good to me," she replied. She stashed her purse under the register and pulled on her smock.

# TWENTY-THREE

Because the field trip wasn't due for a while, Lucy helped Hannah ready the store. Then she went into the bakery to fetch the cinnamon rolls they would be serving at the end. Glaze had spilled on the trays, and Lucy's hands were covered with it by the time she set the trays down in the shop. So she headed for the women's locker room to wash up before meeting the kids and teachers at the back door. In a true gesture of chivalry, Harry eschewed the locker room and instead went into Dave's office to see what was going on in there.

Just inside the locker room door, Lucy stopped short at the sight of Mary Beth hanging up her jacket, while Scott waited on the bench next to her. Both turned as she let out a startled, "Oh!"

Mary Beth turned to Lucy, her expression unreadable. Scott, the eternal kid, waved to Lucy, a goofy smile on his face. Lucy's heart gave a lurch as she realized she had completely forgotten about him.

When she looked back at Mary Beth, she was surprised to see her smiling slightly. "Why didn't you tell me?" she asked, half joking half accusing. For a moment, Lucy thought she was talking about Scott. She opened her mouth to answer, but Mary Beth interrupted her. "This whole time, you could talk to ghosts, and you never said a thing." Mary

Beth shook her head. "Now you get to be famous all by yourself, and the rest of us just get to sit by and be green with envy."

Lucy smiled wanly and then shook her head. "Don't envy me...listen, I'm really sorry about that whole Jerry thing." She paused, searching for the right words. "I wasn't a very good friend to you, and...I'm sorry."

Mary Beth smiled her own crooked smile and then, impulsively, reached over and hugged Lucy. "Don't be. I'm just sorry a jerk like that had to come between us."

Grateful for the reprieve, Lucy returned the hug. When the two women parted, both had tears in their eyes. Laughing, Lucy accepted a tissue from Mary Beth and wiped her eyes. "I'd better go," she sniffed. "We've got a bunch of second-graders coming in any minute now."

Mary Beth nodded. "Me, too...I'll see you on the line."

Lucy watched as Scott followed Mary Beth out the door, and then she walked over to the sinks and washed the glaze that had dried on her hands. When she looked in the mirror, she saw that she was smiling like an idiot. Lucy tried to give herself a dirty look but had to admit that as silly as she felt, she was really happy to have her friend back.

She was drying her hands when she heard voices out in the hallway. Lucy hurriedly threw the paper towel into the trash can by the door and went out to find that the kids had arrived for the field trip.

Two teachers were lining up students along the wall and urging them, somewhat unsuccessfully, to stand quietly. One of the women looked up as Lucy approached and smiled. Then the woman let out a surprised "Oh!" Lucy's stomach did a lurch when she realized the woman had recognized her.

"Aren't you the girl who..." she began, but then caught herself when she realized that the children had chosen that moment to pay attention. "Uh...is taking us around today?" she finished lamely.

"Yes," Lucy answered as the office door opened at the other end of the hallway. She turned to see Dave stepping out, with Mark right behind him. The sight of Mark's uniform sent the children into a frenzy of whispers and giggles. Mark gave them a stern look as he passed them in the hallway, which silenced them effectively. He smiled and winked at her as he passed but said nothing as he made his way to the store. Dave waited as Lucy gave them the welcome speech. Then he gave his own abbreviated welcome before disappearing once more into his office. Lucy herded the kids into the main bakery and began the tour.

Unlike the previous student tour, this one went much more quickly because few second-graders had any questions. In no time, Lucy was leading them into the shop, where Hannah was just setting out napkins and milk.

"What great timing!" she chirped as the children filed in.

Lucy remained at the back of the group as Hannah went into her speech about the function of the shop. Under normal circumstances, she would have enjoyed listening to Hannah's animated lecture, but after today's events, Lucy was keenly aware of how exposed she was, surrounded by all of the shop's windows. She began to inch toward the corner, where she could hide, when Harry appeared. For a brief moment, she entertained the thought that she could just hide behind him. Then she mentally smacked herself in the head. Harry followed, a look of amusement on his face, as she slid into the corner behind the teachers who were listening to Hannah.

Soon it was time to pass out the rolls and milk, so Lucy reluctantly left her corner and went to lend a hand. As she passed out the milk, she looked around, wondering where Mark had gone.

Harry nudged her and pointed out the window. "He's out in his patrol car. They're concerned the press will come here." She shook her head slightly and pursed her lips until they were a thin line.

When all the kids were served, Lucy resumed her place in the corner, where she hoped she could remain unobtrusive. Unfortunately, the teacher who had recognized her earlier chose that moment to come over.

"I just wanted to tell you that the way those reporters treated you was just horrible," she began in an earnest whisper. "I mean, when I first heard the report, I had my own doubts, but now that I've met you, well...I think you're perfectly believable." The young woman gave her a sunny smile as if conferring upon Lucy a great honor.

Lucy gave her a pained smile. "Thanks...I guess." The other woman seemed to sense Lucy's discomfort and excused herself awkwardly to tend to a young girl who was tugging on her skirt, obviously in need of the bathroom.

"Well, you've got supporters, at least," Harry said, trying to be reassuring.

Lucy looked into his hopeful face and wished she could hug him. Instead she turned to help the teachers usher the kids to the sink to wash up.

Dave came in just as the school bus was turning into the parking lot. He said a quick farewell, blushing as the children thanked him enthusiastically. He was so pleased that he stayed to watch as the kids boarded their bus and even waved as they drove off.

Lucy turned to help clear up what was surprisingly little mess. Dave cleared his throat.

"Um, Lucy?" he began, and then he cleared his throat again. "There's been a few phone calls for you...from the press mostly. But some of them are from people who want to know if you can, uh...well, do your psychic thing for them." Dave shifted awkwardly and looked down at his feet. "What do you want me to tell them?"

Lucy was keenly embarrassed that Dave had been forced to play secretary for her. Her face went hot, and she, too, began to stammer. "Gosh, Dave. I'm so sorry. I didn't think about people calling here for me." She shook her head and then pressed the heel of her hand over the ever-present ache over her eye.

It was Dave's turn to blush as Hannah looked on, her face frowning with concern.

"Oh, darn it, you don't need to apologize. I don't mind at all." He gave her a smile, trying to look reassuring. "I just wanted to know what you wanted me to do with the calls, that's all." Then he shrugged. "Maybe we should hire an extra secretary?"

Lucy was mortified that she had put Dave in such an awkward position. Immediately she began to shake her head.

"I should go," she said vehemently. "I should never have brought you this kind of trouble."

Dave and Hannah, and even Harry, began to protest. They closed in around her as if to keep her from leaving. Hannah reached Lucy first and put her arm around her in a motherly hug. Dave took her hand between his own and tried to pat it reassuringly. Crowded out by the others, Harry stood opposite Hannah, his hand wrapped around the spot above Lucy's elbow.

"No one wants you to leave," Hannah murmured soothingly. "In fact, you can't leave. How are we going to keep our eye on you if you're not here?" She pressed her warm, lavender-scented cheek against Lucy's. "Someone has to keep those awful TV people away."

"She's right," Dave added. "You're better off here, and...well...we're better off having you here. So no more talk about leaving, all right?"

Lucy fought the tears that threatened to spill and nodded. Satisfied, Dave gave her hand one last pat.

"I'm going to tell Jean to call in a temp to deal with the phone. You decide what you wanna do and let me know." Lucy nodded. Dave gave her another smile and left.

Hannah gave her another quick hug as Lucy sniffed. "Come on, sweetie. Let's get this place cleaned up."

# TWENTY-FOUR

By the end of the day, Lucy was wondering if they all would have been better off if she had gone home because the majority of the customers who came in weren't there to buy bread. Harry stood by helpless as Lucy spent the day ducking customers' attempts to engage her in conversation. At one point, she was forced to flee the shop as one woman exhausted her entire family tree looking for some long-lost family heirloom. As soon as the woman left, Lucy had another customer proclaiming to be a psychic compatriot. By the time five o'clock rolled around, Lucy was more than ready to go. Luckily, Dave and Mark had the same idea; Mark was pulling his patrol car up to the door just as Dave walked in to lock up the store.

"Mark's gonna take you home and make sure them reporters don't bother you any," Dave said gruffly. His face was beet red, and he seemed out of breath. Lucy set aside her own worries and hurried up to him.

"Are you OK, Dave?" Lucy asked. The tone in her voice made Hannah turn and look at Dave sharply.

Dave looked down at the keys in his hand, tears in his eyes. "I guess I was just hoping you were the other kind of psychic."

Lucy went over and put her arms around him. "I'm so sorry. If I could talk to Mrs. Landerkin for you, it would be the very first thing I'd do."

Dave turned and gave Lucy a big hug. "I know you would, honey. I know you would."

Just then, Mark's car pulled as close to the door as he dared. Dave patted Lucy's back and gave her one last squeeze. "You go now. We'll see you tomorrow."

Lucy kissed Dave's cheek and smiled as the older man blushed furiously. "Thank you, Dave...for everything."

Dave waved away her thanks as Hannah handed Lucy her coat and purse.

Mark waited at the car door, his eyes scanning the end of the bakery's driveway. "It doesn't look like they've stuck around. There were only a few vans parked out on the highway, but Acco's moved most of them on."

Lucy was glad but still nervous about what she was going to find at home. But it was just as Mark had said—only two vans were left at the end of the bakery's drive. Unfortunately, both drivers started to follow Lucy home. They made a strange procession as they drove through the small town of Paris, Ohio. At her home, Lucy was grateful to see that many of the news vans and reporters had gone as well. Deputy Acco waited at the end of her driveway to wave them in, only a handful of cameras and reporters at his back.

When they came to a stop, Lucy ran into the house as quickly as she could to avoid answering any more questions.

Inside, the house was relatively empty of ghosts. Only Harry, Michael, and Whitney were in the living room. Whitney hovered near the sofa, scanning for news of Lucy on the television, while Michael and Harry consulted the list of the missing. Lucy waited, hanging up her coat and dropping her purse, as Mark walked to the back of the house to make sure no reporters were lurking outside the back door. When he was satisfied, he returned to the living room and looked around.

"Is there anyone here?" he asked, meaning ghosts.

"Just three: Harry, Michael, and Whitney," Lucy answered. "Why?"

"Which one's the publicist?" he asked.

Whitney looked up from her channel surfing and glanced at Lucy.

"Whitney was a publicist," she answered. "Why?"

Mark moved over to the window and looked out at the vans still parked in front of Lucy's house. "Dave has been getting phone calls at the bakery. Some from reporters, but more of them are from people looking for help." He turned and sat down in a threadbare rocker and looked to where he thought Whitney might be. "Someone needs to figure out how to handle not just the reporters, but those people, too."

Whitney looked thoughtful. Lucy was struck by the change in the young woman. Personally she seemed very unpleasant, but Lucy would bet that Whitney had been very good at her job.

"Well, from what I can gather from Pretty Boy here and the television, your best bet would be to set up a website to handle the people looking for someone. The press will go away as soon as something else happens." Whitney went back to flipping the channels on the television. "Just pray someone gets kidnapped or a politician gets caught with his pants down."

Lucy relayed Whitney's suggestion to Mark, who looked thoughtful. "A website is a good idea. My brother knows how to put one together. I'll see if he can come over tomorrow." Mark pushed himself out of the chair and stretched. "You should get some rest. I'll talk to Joe about picking up a computer for you."

Lucy started to protest, but Mark put up his hand. "Don't. I'm doing it anyway," he said, and then he walked out.

Whitney watched the young cop as he left. "He's hot," she remarked. Then she went back to the television.

Lucy went into the kitchen and grabbed a carrot out of the refrigerator. Harry followed her and sat down at the table. "I'm sorry," he said quietly. "If I hadn't convinced you to help us, you wouldn't be suffering this terrible exposure right now."

Lucy shrugged. "You keep saying that, but honestly, I think something would have happened anyway. So it's sooner rather than later."

"Still, I hope we can figure out how to ameliorate your situation before it gets beyond our meager capabilities," he replied.

"We will," Lucy assured him. "With so many people willing to help—even Whitney—I think everything will be fine." Lucy finished her carrot and washed her hands at the sink. "I think I'm going to go up and rest for a bit."

Harry got up to hug her. Lucy marveled at the feeling of his arms around her. She pressed her face against his jacket and inhaled a faint yet strange scent of dog and tobacco. After a very long moment, Harry dropped his arms and held her at arm's length. Lucy looked up into his gentle smile.

"Go rest."

# TWENTY-FIVE

Though several news vans were still out front, Lucy had a much easier time getting through them and off to work than she had the past few days. Deputy Acco still followed her and parked his patrol car at the entrance to the bakery's drive to keep the press from straying onto the property. Lucy drove around the building and parked next to Hannah's car.

She went in. The day was relatively normal, with little talk about ghosts, the press, or visitors wanting more than just bread. Paris had moved on from the news that they had a minor celebrity in their midst, and life for most residents resumed its normal course.

Lucy finished up her day and was just punching out when Mary Beth walked in from the factory.

"Hey, Luce," she said, smiling. Scott made faces at Lucy over her shoulder. "Can I ask you something?"

Lucy did her best to ignore Scott. "Sure," she answered. "What's up?"

Mary Beth thought for a moment. "I know people have probably been hounding you like crazy...and I promised myself I wouldn't bother you, but—" Mary Beth paused, unsure how to ask her question. "I guess, I just wanted to know if you knew anything about Scott. He left so long ago, and we've never heard from him, so I was wondering if there was anything you can find out."

Lucy looked past Mary Beth to Scott, who'd fallen still upon hearing his sister's question. He stared at her and then looked at Lucy.

"Um, let me look into it, and I'll let you know what I find, OK?" Lucy offered.

Mary Beth relaxed, relieved that her former friend had not turned her away. "Thanks, Lucy. Anything would be great."

Lucy nodded. Then she left, with a subtle look at Scott, who followed.

In the car on the way home, Lucy explained to Scott what would happen if she told Mary Beth about his death. "...and you'll turn into a bunch of white lights and then disappear, forever."

Scott sat silent next to her, his face pensive. "I don't want her to always wonder what happened, you know? I mean, it could be cool on the other side, but it's seriously cool here. But you should probably tell her." Scott looked at Lucy, his face sad. "I like how things are, though... you know?"

Lucy nodded. "I know," she said sadly and turned the car around. She wasn't surprised when Scott disappeared. She assumed he would be spending as much time as possible with his sister before he moved on.

She made it back to the bakery in time to see Mary Beth walking to her car. She stopped in surprise as Lucy pulled in beside her. Scott looked on sadly.

"Do you have a second?" Lucy asked as she got out.

"Sure," Mary Beth threw her bag into her front seat and followed Lucy to a bench just outside the bakery store. Scott trailed behind them, stopping just short of the bench to watch his sister.

"I wanted to let you know what I know about Scott," she said gently. Mary Beth looked surprised. "If you know what happens to him, he'll move on. I only see people who are among the missing, and when their family finds out, they stop being missing, and I can't see them anymore."

"So you're telling me that Scott *is* missing?" Mary Beth asked.

Both Scott and Lucy nodded.

"And if you tell me, he'll go to heaven, but if you don't he'll stay here?"

Lucy and Scott nodded again.

Mary Beth sat silently for a moment, and Lucy had to wonder how Scott was still there. Either Mary Beth didn't quite believe it, or Scott's presence meant that the families weren't the ones keeping the ghosts from moving on.

Mary Beth seemed to make a decision. "I want him to go to heaven," she said firmly. "I can't be selfish and keep him here with me."

"Are you sure?" Lucy asked. When Mary Beth nodded, Lucy told her the story of Scott's death. By the end, both women were crying.

"Is he gone now?" Mary Beth asked through her tears. Lucy looked over and was surprised that Scott still stood there.

"I'm not going to go," he said stubbornly. "I'm going to wait for her."

Lucy laughed as she wiped the tears from her face. "He's still here. He says he's going to wait for you."

Mary Beth started laughing, too. "That sounds just like him. He was always waiting for me, except for that last time." Scott moved over and put his arms around his sister. Mary Beth's eyes widened. "Oh my gosh, he *is* here!"

Scott let go as Mary Beth reached over and gave Lucy a warm hug.

"Thank you so much for this. I would never have known what happened if it weren't for you."

"I'm glad he's staying," Lucy said as she returned her hug, and then said good-bye, leaving the siblings to each other. Scott was beaming as Lucy drove away.

At home, Mark and a younger version of Mark were waiting in Lucy's driveway. Surprisingly, all the news vans and reporters had gone. Lucy pulled up alongside Mark's patrol car.

"Wow!" she exclaimed. "How did you get rid of them?"

"Wasn't me," Mark shrugged. "Something bigger must have happened." Mark turned to his brother. "Do you remember Joe? He was a couple of years behind us." Joe waved a hand and smiled.

Lucy smiled back. "I remember. Hi, Joe."

Mark picked up a box, and Joe carried a bag filled with smaller boxes. Both headed for Lucy's front door. "I hope you don't mind, but I went ahead and picked up a computer and some things you'll need to go online."

Lucy followed with a pensive Scott trailing behind her. "Let me know what I owe you," she said as she moved past them to unlock the door.

Inside Joe and Mark set to work putting Lucy's new computer system together. Harry, Michael, and Whitney appeared and stood by to watch as Lucy went upstairs to change.

When she came back downstairs, Joe was sitting in front of a new laptop, already entering data from Lucy's list.

"Wow, that was fast," she remarked. "But I don't have Internet service here."

"I got you a prepaid broadband USB card until you have it installed," Joe answered. "But you might not need to use it for a while. Your neighbor didn't put a password on his WIFI, so I'm piggybacking on his instead."

"Is that legal?" Lucy asked.

Joe looked at his brother and then at Lucy. "Umm...not really no and not really yes. It's his account, but it looks like he has DSL, so he's not going to notice. Are you really good friends?"

Lucy thought about it. "We're really good neighbors. I don't see him very much since he works nights and I work days. But he's a good guy."

"Then we're cool," Joe said with finality. Mark still looked conflicted but said nothing as his brother worked on Lucy's new website. Whitney watched over his shoulder, making suggestions he couldn't hear.

"Do we know why the news vans are gone?" Lucy asked.

"Some kids have gone missing in some town not far from here. They think it's a serial killer," Whitney answered without looking away. "That's always going to pull in the press."

"Oh my God!" Lucy cried. "That's awful!" Mark and Joe glanced at her oddly, unused to overhearing one-sided conversations. Joe actually looked a little alarmed but turned back to the screen without comment.

Whitney glanced at her. "Just what you needed, though," she said, and then she looked back at the computer. "You know she's going to need a web administrator to run this, right? And you're going to need to set up a separate login for law enforcement," she said to Joe, who was blissfully unaware that he was being given orders.

"Um, he can't hear you, Whitney," Lucy said. She looked at Joe. "Whitney says I'm going to need a web administrator and a separate login for law enforcement."

"Duh," he replied without looking away.

Whitney threw her hands up in the air and disappeared from the room.

They spent the rest of the evening working on the website, entering all the information Lucy and Harry already had. Joe sat with Lucy and showed her how to do her own entries as more ghosts came for help. Harry also watched Joe, trying to learn, but at a distinct disadvantage because he had no knowledge of computers.

By the end of the evening, even the ghosts were tired. Lucy saw Joe and Mark out the door, thanking them effusively for all their help. She took a dose of the headache medicine George had found for her and went upstairs to get ready for bed.

She stepped out of the bathroom to find Harry sitting on her bed, his hands dangling limply between his knees, his face drawn and tired. Lucy wondered if he felt fatigue the way she did or if it was just a state of mind.

"Are you OK?" she asked.

Harry looked up and smiled. "I should be asking you that," he said. "You worked harder than any of us today."

Lucy shook her head. "I didn't, though. Everyone is working hard."

Harry stood, took her hands in his and guided her to the bed. Lucy sat, moving over when Harry sat next to her. His expression was serious, but he raised his hand to brush her hair from her face, letting it linger against her cheek. Lucy yearned to feel his lips against hers, and her heart surged when he leaned over and obliged. She was breathless when he finally pulled away and took her face in his hands.

"You should rest," he said.

"Will you stay with me?" Lucy asked, fearful that he might decline. She needn't have worried.

"Of course," he answered.

He lay next to her, his arms wrapped around her, his chest pressed firmly against her back. Lucy felt him rest his cheek against her as she closed her eyes. She fought sleep, wanting to relish every moment with him, but it wasn't long before she was lost to her exhaustion.

# TWENTY-SIX

The next few days fell into a routine, and Lucy hoped that life would soon go back to normal—or as normal as possible, given that ghosts continued to show up on a daily basis. Harry's confidence grew on the computer, and he was able to enter most of the new arrivals himself. Mark helped by contacting various law-enforcement agencies, with mixed results, to inform them that information regarding a case local to them could be found on the website. Most calls were unsuccessful, but once in a while, an open-minded investigator was willing to give it a try. Some ghosts could not be helped because of language barriers, and Lucy agonized over turning them away.

The hardest part was saying good-bye to the ghosts she'd become friends with. First Shelley and Jeannie, then George, and now it was Michael's turn. Once Lucy's tip had been verified, the Park Service had dispatched a team to the location she'd provided. They finally found Michael's body wedged in a rock formation several hundred feet from the trail he'd fallen from. When his sister, Rebecca, was notified, Michael's time with Lucy and the others ended. And Lucy's reputation grew.

Though reporters were no longer camped outside, the phone still rang with offers from various news and entertainment producers wanting Lucy to appear and either answer questions or show viewers how she helped the missing pass on. Because neither Harry nor Whitney could help with these, it fell to Lucy to handle those calls. There were so many, though, that after a while, she stopped answering and screened them through her answering machine instead.

It was early Saturday morning when Lucy heard Detective Brown's voice come on the machine. "Hi, Lucy. It's Matt Brown. There's a show that's been following up on the murders down here, and they want to interview you about your ability and the work you're trying to do. Before you say no, they're from the Discovery Channel, and they sound pretty legitimate. Give me a call when you get this message so I can clear up any concerns you might have. Thanks, Lucy. Bye."

Lucy was already shaking her head when the message ended. "I'm not going on TV."

Whitney snorted. "Yeah, you're not exactly TV ready, if you know what I mean."

Harry looked thoughtful.

"What?" Whitney asked.

"I'm thinking it might not be a bad idea," he ventured. "It could promote the website and maybe help legitimize Lucy's ability with the various police agencies."

"I don't want to be on TV," Lucy replied. "It's hard enough now that everyone knows what I can...do...I don't want to make it a 'thing.' I just want to go back to my boring old life when this is done."

Harry and Whitney looked at each other, their expressions identical. Lucy looked from one to the other.

"What?"

"I don't think that's possible, Lucy," he said. "You've been identified as a resource, not just for the living...but for the dead, too. As long as people go missing, they'll be coming to you for help."

"But we have the website now," Lucy protested. "You don't even need me to use it."

"It won't work that way," Whitney chimed in. "We need a human spokesperson, someone to convince our families and the cops that we're really here."

"But I'm not convincing," Lucy said.

"No, you're not," Whitney agreed. "But you're all we have. Unless someone else comes along, you're it."

Lucy looked from Harry to Whitney and back. Harry's expression was hopeful and encouraging, while Whitney just looked tired. Lucy knew she couldn't let them down. She dropped the argument as the spot over her eye began to ache.

"So this is it, huh?" Lucy said quietly. "This is what I'm supposed to do."

For once, Whitney looked sympathetic. "I know it sucks. But if we do it right, you can still live a normal life...well, mostly normal."

Lucy rubbed her forehead and went into the kitchen to take some pain medication before it turned worse. Rather than return to the living room, she stepped out the back door and sat on the step facing the fields behind her house.

So much had been going on that Lucy hadn't stopped to think about what had happened in such a short period of time. Never one to surround herself with lots of friends, she found she now had more people around her than she'd known in her entire life, even if they were dead. If she was really honest with herself, she could admit that before Harry had shown up, she had been lonely. And as much as she could blame Jerry for her isolation, she knew in her heart that it had been her own fault. Even if young people were short on the ground in Paris, Ohio, there were plenty of others who would have been happy to see her. And the ghosts were definitely happy to see her.

Lucy smiled. It felt good to be needed. And it felt good to have Harry around. Her smile faltered as she thought of the day when he would go on. She knew he'd taken his name off the list so that he could stay and help her, but to make him stay with her was selfish. And it would be selfish to prevent anyone else from moving on.

Lucy put her own feelings aside and got up to return Detective Brown's call.

# TWENTY-SEVEN

The production company worked fast, and it was only a week later when Lucy made the one-hour drive to one of the nicer hotels in downtown Columbus, where the production company had rented rooms. A production assistant stood waiting for her at the entrance and indicated that the valet would park her car for her.

"Hi, Lucy? I'm Trish Goldman," she said, stepping forward to shake Lucy's hand. "We're right this way. Did you have any trouble finding the hotel?"

"Nope," Lucy replied as she and Harry followed the young woman into the lobby. The production assistant led Lucy down several hallways to a section of the hotel that looked like meeting rooms. She stopped and escorted Lucy into a small room that had been decorated to look like a cross between a library and an office. There was a wall of cameras with two chairs placed opposite each other.

"You'll be in here first to do your one-on-one with Robert. Then we'll take you to the panel for the group interview. OK?"

Lucy nodded and took the seat the young woman indicated. An aging makeup boy hovered around her, adjusting her hair and powdering the shine from her forehead.

A minute later, the host entered. He looked familiar though Lucy didn't watch much television. She smiled as he stopped in the doorway to look through his notes. Then he glanced up and returned her smile.

"Hi, Lucy, I'm Robert Morrison. You doing OK?" he asked as he sat in the chair across from her. Whitney took up a position next to him, while Harry stood behind Lucy. "Are you nervous?"

"A little," she admitted.

"Don't be," he said. His voice was clearly practiced at sounding warm and reassuring. "It's worse to be in front of an audience. Just pretend we're having a conversation. The key is simply to keep looking at me."

"OK."

The crew made light and camera adjustments. Then from the back of the room, the segment producer called for the camera to start rolling and announced the date, time, and title of the show.

Robert's face affected a serious expression. "When did you know you had psychic ability?"

Lucy inadvertently mirrored his seriousness. "I don't think I'm psychic. I just recently found that I could see and hear people who had died, but their families didn't know they had died. Since few people in my town go missing, I don't know when it actually began."

There was a long pause before he asked his next question. "And how far do your alleged abilities extend? Can you tell me what I'm thinking?"

Lucy shook her head. "No."

"How about something from my past or present?"

"No."

"So you don't claim to have the ability to read people in the traditional sense."

"No. In fact, I don't know anything about the ghosts who contact me other than what they tell me and how they look."

"Some might say that you are, in fact, not psychic at all."

Lucy looked thoughtful. "I agree with them," she answered. "I don't think I am psychic. I can't read minds or make things move, and I don't have any awareness of people who have died but haven't moved on unless they are missing. I think people might label me a medium more than anything else."

Robert shifted in his seat and looked through his papers. "So walk me through the process. How do you let people know you have information about their family members?"

"I have a set of questions I ask the people who come to me, like their name and where they lived and how they died. Then I try to track down their families. Some keep in touch, and some don't, so sometimes it's difficult."

"Tell me about Jeannie Allen and Shelly Martini."

Lucy recounted the events of the previous few months. She tried to stay matter-of-fact, but at times her voice would catch at the memory of their terrible ordeal.

"The North Carolina State Police put great store in your ability."

"All I wanted to do was help them."

"You received payment for your information, didn't you?"

"I was given a reward for the information I provided, yes."

"So this 'ability' has provided you with an income?"

"No. I used part of the reward to buy a computer, and I donated the rest to the National Center for Missing and Exploited Children."

"How much was donated?"

"Almost eighteen thousand dollars."

The interviewer raised his eyebrows. "What about the other four thousand?"

"I used some for the computer, and the rest went to pay taxes on that money."

"And what about the other missing cases you've solved? How much did they pay you?"

"Nothing."

"You don't ask for any compensation for the service you provide?"

Lucy shook her head. "No."

"Can I ask why?"

Lucy thought for a moment. "I guess I don't really feel like I'm doing anything worth charging for. It's like seeing someone out and about and they tell me to say hi to someone for them. I wouldn't expect money for that. I'm just passing on a message."

"Other mediums charge for their services, sometimes quite a bit."

Lucy shrugged. "People are willing to do all kinds of things for money. For me it's not about the money. I just want to help them if I can."

"You told our producer earlier that you did not want to appear on television. Yet you're here now."

"I really don't want to be on television. I'm only here to answer your questions and to ask people to check the website we've set up if someone they love is missing."

"And how much does it cost to access the website?"

"Nothing. It's free."

"So how does it work? If someone comes up to your door and asks you for help, what happens?"

"If they were asking me to talk to their parent or someone who has already died, nothing happens. I can't help them. But if they have someone they can't find and want to know if they are part of the group of... well, I guess they're spirits...that have already come to me, then I can try to help them. But we try to make the first contact."

"And how do you do that?"

Lucy glanced up at Whitney, who nodded slightly.

"If a spirit comes to me and can give me information on themselves and their family, I try to find the best means of contact, like their home phone or a hotline number. Depending on who I reach, I give as much information as I have to let them know what's happened."

"And do they believe you?"

"Not at first, no. But eventually they do. It can't be easy to hear that the person you are missing, that you love and had hope that they would return is dead. I try not to take it personally when someone doesn't believe me." Lucy gave him a pointed look. "Would *you* believe me?"

He smiled. "I would now."

The segment producer called a cut as Robert stood.

"We're going into the other room in a moment," he said. "We have a woman whose son seems to have the same ability as you do, plus some debunking experts as well as other mediums."

Lucy nodded and stood to follow the producer out.

Down the hall was a smaller banquet room that had been darkened. In the center of the room stood a semicircle of chairs lit by standing lights. Lucy took the seat the producer pointed to and sat quietly as others were brought in.

The boy was accompanied by his mother, and Lucy mourned for him. He was small and thin and looked very tired. They were followed by two older gentlemen, a younger woman who looked very comfortable and very happy to be there, and an older woman who looked extremely bored.

Harry took up a position next to Lucy, while Whitney remained across from her near the producer but still within her line of sight. Lucy's breath caught as Detective Brown, Mark, and Joe slid into the room at the end and took a seat behind the cameras. Joe pulled out the laptop and set it up on his lap. She wondered why they were there but was grateful to see them. Her head was starting to ache, and she regretted not bringing anything to take for it. She desperately wanted to rub at the spot over her eye but didn't want to ruin her makeup. They waited as they were each fitted with microphones and the sound quality was checked.

When everyone was ready, Robert took the center chair, facing them.

"I have a series of questions that I'll be addressing. Most will be directed at one of you specifically. I'll say your name so you'll know when they are for you."

Everyone nodded and waited in silence. Lucy startled to see the ghost of an older man appear next to the boy, who stiffened when the ghost leaned over to whisper into the boy's ear. Lucy glanced over at Whitney, who was watching the exchange with concern.

When the producer called for taping to begin, Robert began with a series of introductions. The two older men were identified as the skeptics and debunkers, while the women were introduced as the mediums. Then the boy was introduced as another possible medium.

Robert's first question went to one of the gentlemen. Right from the get-go, the skeptic launched into a diatribe condemning the mediums as mentally ill, schizophrenic, greedy charlatans. The other skeptic jumped in while the mediums waved them off like flies. Lucy and the boy sat in silence while Robert tried to regain control of the interview.

Lucy watched as the boy's expression turned stricken with each comment from his ghost. She was wondering about the extent of his ability when she caught him glancing over at Harry, whose hand tightened in hers. He had noticed the boy's glance, and she could tell he was worried.

When the room was settled again, Robert posed to her the question of the presence of ghosts. Lucy hadn't been paying attention.

"I'm sorry, what did you say?"

"I was asking if any ghosts are present right now," he said warmly.

Lucy was about to answer when the younger medium spoke up.

"There is an older woman present right now. Maybe someone's mother?" she offered.

The two skeptics snorted but remained silent. It was the older medium who spoke up.

"No, there isn't anyone here. There's too much interference for spirit to come through."

Robert looked over at Lucy. "What about you, Lucy? Is there anyone here?"

Lucy hesitated, taking strength from Harry, who squeezed her hand again. "Yes. There are three spirits here." She startled as the little boy's ghost snapped to attention and glared at her. "There are two spirits here with me, and there is one next to the boy."

"And who are they? What kind of impressions do you have of them?"

"Harry was the first spirit who contacted me, and Whitney arrived a little while ago. They've been helping me. I don't know who the other spirit is, but I think he came with the boy."

"You're saying there is a ghost with Daniel?"

Lucy nodded. "He's an older man, tall, thin with sandy brown hair that's receding." Her eyes widened as the ghost approached. The air felt like it was charged with electricity, and there was a faint smell of ozone. Harry stood and placed himself slightly in front of her.

"Can you tell me his name?"

Lucy shook her head. "Not unless he tells me. Otherwise I don't know who he is."

Daniel's ghost stopped and looked at her with uncertainty.

"So if you can see him, that means he is a missing person, correct?"

"Yes. They are the only spirits I can see."

"Can you describe him further?"

Lucy started to nod when the ghost flew at her, knocking her from the chair. To the rest of the room, it looked like Lucy had been violently pushed to the floor by an unseen force.

Harry and Whitney reacted instinctively, trying to put themselves between Lucy and the angry spirit. Whitney's power was weak, however, and she stood by helplessly as Harry moved to cover Lucy as best he could. The other ghost was stronger though and forced Harry aside. He put his hands around Lucy's throat. All the room saw was Lucy thrashing on the floor, her face turning red. Mark and Detective Brown had rushed forward to help her but were also pushed back by the ghost. As his hand moved from her throat, Lucy gasped, "Daniel." The others sat in shock as violent red marks arose in a ring around her neck.

Whitney turned and looked at the boy, who sat paralyzed with fear as he watched Lucy's eyes go blank.

"Richard," Daniel whispered. "His name is Richard, and he killed people."

Daniel's ghost released Lucy, turned to stare at the boy, and then slowly stood and walked toward him.

"What's his last name?" Joe asked quietly from the back of the room.

"Rader. His name is Richard Lee Rader. His body's in his old hunting cabin." Suddenly the room erupted as the ghost flew toward the boy. Detective Brown pulled his phone from his belt and started to dial frantically as Joe's fingers flew across the keyboard. Lucy and Whitney flew forward and covered Daniel as the angry ghost tried to attack the boy. Daniel's mother screamed. An unseen hand shoved her aside while Lucy wrapped her body around the boy. Richard's arms pushed between them as he tried to pull the boy away from Lucy by his shirt. The knit tore, revealing Daniel's thin chest. Lucy gasped at the scattering of black and blue marks that painted the boy's pale skin. Lucy tightened her hold on Daniel, sending Richard into a fury. He rained blows on her head and back as Whitney tried to pull him away. In her fear, her strength grew, and she and Harry pulled Richard away from Lucy and the boy. Lights came crashing down, and papers flew as Richard Rader vented his anger on the room. Lucy and Daniel's eyes went wide as Richard's form filled with hundreds and then thousands of fiery red lights. Richard let out an ear-splitting scream as his body burst into a fireball.

The room went silent as papers floated to the floor.

"Yes, Mrs. Rader," Joe said quietly into his cell phone. "He's moved on. Thank you."

Detective Brown and Mark pushed themselves off the floor and moved to help Lucy up. She pulled Daniel with her, and then hugged him as he started to cry.

"It's OK, Daniel," she whispered through the pain in her throat. "He's gone now, and he won't ever come back. You did really well."

She found that she too was crying.

"I don't know what you people are trying to pull, but that was a load of bullshit!" one of the skeptics exclaimed, pulling his microphone off his shirt. The younger medium responded by launching into an erroneous recounting of the events that had just occurred, while the older woman sat and glared at her. The other skeptic remained in his chair, a stunned look on his face.

Mark checked Lucy's neck while Detective Brown examined Daniel. Daniel's mother had managed to push herself off the floor and was sobbing next to her son.

"They told us he was autistic and schizophrenic. They gave him all kinds of horrible pills that made him sick, and all along it was that horrible man!" she cried. "I'm so sorry, Danny. We should have listened to you."

Harry knelt in front of Daniel. "Can you see me?" he asked, and Daniel nodded. "We're going to protect you from now on," Harry said. "We won't let anyone else like that bad man near you, OK?"

Daniel nodded again and then pressed his face into his mother's stomach, his shoulders shaking with his sobs.

Whitney stepped forward. "I'll go with him."

Harry and Lucy looked at her in surprise. "Are you sure?" Harry asked.

Whitney nodded. "We can't find my family at all, and I'm pretty sure Lucy here isn't going to be doing any more TV interviews. Besides, you'll know where to find me if anything comes up." Whitney knelt in front of Daniel. "I'm going to take care of you, OK?" Daniel gave her a teary smile and nodded.

Lucy was touched at Whitney's kindness to the little boy. Clearly she'd underestimated the other woman. She mouthed "Good-bye" to her as Detective Brown pulled her away to a waiting paramedic.

Whitney nodded and smiled, her hand on Daniel's shoulder.

# TWENTY-EIGHT

Because it was the weekend, Lucy had the next couple of days to recover. She went back to work with a necklace of bruises, sending Hannah off on a tangent condemning everyone even remotely related to the show. Luckily it was getting colder, and she could hide them under turtleneck sweaters while she worked in the store.

Things seemed to have calmed down since the taping, and with Whitney gone, Lucy felt shy and uncomfortable with only Harry around. But just when things seemed normal, all hell broke loose.

One night, Lucy awoke to a splitting headache and a cacophony of noise unlike the previous invasion by the press. She rolled out of bed and stepped to the window to see not only news vans but more than a hundred people, both living and dead, filling her yard and the street.

She heard a knock on her front door and went downstairs to see Harry opening it for Joe. Mark and Deputy Acco remained outside to move the press back and to keep anyone from approaching the house. Unfortunately, the dead had wandered inside, and Harry was trying to clear the crowded living room.

"What's going on?" she asked Joe.

"Apparently someone leaked a video of that ghost beating you up during the Discovery Channel interview. It's gone viral," Joe answered as he booted up Lucy's computer.

Lucy walked over to the computer screen, watching herself get thrown out of her chair and then writhing on the floor like she was having an epileptic fit. The audio wasn't very good, so Daniel's voice couldn't be heard, but the camera swung in his direction and caught him mouthing the name of the ghost who had been tormenting him. Lucy startled when she burst back into the frame to cover Daniel with her body. Then the room erupted in a whirlwind of overturning chairs and flying papers. Sparks flew as the lights crashed to the floor. The look on the skeptics' faces might have been funny if it weren't for the terror on Daniel's face. The camera skewed as a light fell in front of it, and then it righted to a scene of utter calm.

"It's all over the Internet, and the visits to the website have gone through the roof," Joe said, pulling up the website. "I think the people out there are hoping you can talk to the dead for them."

Lucy pressed both hands to her eyes. "There's more than alive people here."

Joe looked concerned for a minute and then turned back to the computer. "Well, you and your Harry friend are going to have to deal with them. I can take care of the living ones."

"How are you going to do that?" she asked as she stepped into the kitchen to take some pain medicine.

"I'm setting up a section on the website that people can fill in if they are looking for someone. Sort of the reverse of just listing the people who are missing. That way you don't have to try to help all those people one-on-one. Oh, and Mark called the bakery and told them you were trapped at home. They said for you to stay put. Mark thinks you should stay inside until they get everyone to leave."

"That's a great idea," Lucy replied. "If you don't need me, I'm going back upstairs to lie down."

Joe glanced in her direction. "You don't look so good."

"I don't feel so good," she answered. She slowly made her way back to her bedroom.

Lucy pulled the heavier curtains across her window to block out the light and crawled into bed.

She felt a cool hand on her head and opened her eyes to see Harry smiling down at her.

"Are you feeling all right?" he asked quietly.

Lucy smiled weakly. "I will be. I just need to rest."

"I'm going to check on Whitney and Daniel to make sure they aren't being bombarded like we are here.

Lucy tried to nod. "OK."

Harry leaned over and pressed his lips against her forehead. Lucy sighed and closed her eyes. A few minutes later, just as she was on the verge of sleep, she felt him lie down next to her, his body following the curve of hers, his lips in her hair.

When she opened her eyes again, she was alone. The window showed a setting sun. She could hear the television on downstairs and wondered if Joe had stayed the whole time.

There was a sharp pain behind her eye as she stood up and crossed to the bathroom to brush the foul taste from her mouth.

She could hear a faint knock at the front door and wandered downstairs to answer it. As she descended the steps, she was surprised to see Jerry standing in the middle of her living room. Joe had beat her to the front door. Both Joe and Jerry were unaware that the room was filled to capacity with ghosts.

"What are you doing here?" she asked, too tired to argue and too sore to care.

"Uncle Dave sent me to see if you needed anything," he said, trying to sound amiable. Lucy knew it was a lie. Jerry was the last person Dave would send. "There's a million people trying to see you," he continued. "He thought you might need help,"

Lucy watched his eyes cut to the side and was about to challenge his claim when another knock sounded at the door. Joe let in a young woman who looked vaguely familiar.

"Hey, Lucy," Joe said, as he led the young woman into the living room. "I know Mark said not to let anyone else in, but I thought this one might be important. She says her name is Anna. Anna Truman?"

Lucy was about to reply when a searing pain shot through her head. She felt a sharp snap like a rubber band breaking deep behind her eye, and then she felt the side of her face go numb. The last thing she saw was Harry's features on his sister's face widening in shock. Then everything went dark.

"Oh my God!" Joe cried as Lucy crumpled to the floor. Jerry stood there in shock as Anna ran to Joe's side.

"Let me look at her," she said, her voice calm and professional. "I'm a physician."

Joe left Lucy to Anna and ran into the kitchen to call 911. "Hey, Jerry," he called back. "See if Mark is still outside."

Jerry remained still, staring at Lucy as Anna began to perform CPR, unaware that the ghosts surrounding her were shouting instructions. Anna moved to chest compressions as Harry flew in and rushed to Lucy's side.

"Hey! Jerry! Can you hear me?" Joe called from the kitchen. "I need you, dude."

In a daze, Jerry looked up and around the room. "Who are all these people?"

As a unit, all the ghosts turned and looked at Jerry in surprise.

"Oh my God," Jerry said as his face went white. "Oh my God, oh my God." He gave a final look of horror at Lucy and then fled out the back door with the ghosts following.

Joe shouted the address into the phone and then left the handset on the counter to run to the front door as Mark was letting himself in.

Anna sat back on her heels, her expression sad. Her brother laid his cheek against Lucy's forehead and cried silent tears.

Anna looked up at Mark, who stared at Lucy in shock.

"She's gone."

# TWENTY-NINE

Hundreds of people attended Lucy's funeral, living and dead alike. Detective Brown sat with Daniel and his mother, Whitney close by Daniel's side. Mary Beth sat with Scott, while Mark and Joe had Harry's sister with them. No one had seen Jerry since the night Lucy died.

When the service was done, only a select few were admitted to the burial. Dave and Mary Beth escorted a sobbing Hannah as Mark, Joe, and Anna followed. Deputy Acco was there to make sure the uninvited stayed away.

The burial service was brief, and Lucy's closest friends lingered at the grave site.

Anna broke the silence. "I can't believe I was too late."

Everyone turned to look at her. "I've been in Uganda for the last few years working with Médecins Sans Frontières," she said quietly. "I was in South Africa when I heard about Lucy. I looked at the website, but I didn't see anything. I was hoping she could tell me something about my brother."

Mark looked on as Joe handed her Harry's notes. It was a list of all the ghosts they'd met so far. Anna wouldn't recognize the handwriting, but at the very end, it changed. In handwriting completely unlike the rest of the list, someone had written Harry's name, Anna's name, and the circumstances of Harry's death.

"Oh!" she cried as Harry searched his sister's face. "I think this is him. She did know him."

Harry felt the heat of a gaze on his skin and looked up. Lucy stood at the edge of her own grave, smiling at him. She was surrounded by a halo of light that felt both warm and loving.

"Are you ready to go?" she asked, her voice echoing from the distance of every minute lived by every soul across all existence.

Harry's heart filled with an immeasurable joy as he moved to her side. Lucy reached out and took his hands, iridescent tears spilling from her eyes. Together they began to glow as the wind whipped around them, sending flower petals raining over the group of the living. Harry moved to embrace Lucy, and together they burst into a million stars.

# ACKNOWLEDGMENTS:

Though writing is a solitary effort, many people are involved in the process of taking that writing and turning it into a published book. I'd like to thank two of those people, Susan Dawnson and Rosann Stein Johnson for their keen eyes, loving criticism, and unfailing support.

Other titles by K. Wiley Sider:

**The Things That Fall Away**
**Solitary**
**Servant**
**Boy Toy, Book One of the Dead Husbands Series**

Learn more about the author at:

www.kwileysider.com
www.facebook.com/kwileysider

and on Twitter at:
@kwileysider

www.ingramcontent.com/pod-product-compliance
Lightning Source LLC
Chambersburg PA
CBHW071145170626
46809CB00002B/775